I0551769

Loyalty II

Loyalty Is Everything

A Novel By
Tammy Capri

Published by: Nu Class Publications

Editor: Carla M. Dean of U Can Mark My Word
        Editorial Services

Model: Gregory Talley

Photographer: Cal Akbar

ISBN-13: 978-0-9891342-0-0
ISBN-10: 0-9891342-0-2

Printed in USA

Submit whole sale orders to TammyCapri@yahoo.com

DEDICATION

To a brother who was called home in the midst of his prime. You will forever be remembered, and I will always cherish our memories.

Rest in Paradise Michael Lewis

TAMMY CAPRI

ACKNOWLEDGMENTS

First, I would like to thank God for the many blessings he has bestowed upon me.

 Thanks to my family: my husband, children, mother, my mommy # 2, father, my in-laws, aunts, cousins and friends. Thank you for the endless motivation. You all are my biggest cheerleaders, and your support and encouragement goes a long way.

Thanks to my team, Nu Class Publications, for all the hard work you put in. Without your dedication, I would probably need a strait-jacket. ☺

Thanks to Carla M. Dean, the editor, and all the proofreaders who worked on this book.

And thanks to everyone who has ever picked up anyone of my novels. To Mrs. Denise Corporal, the most dedicated reader that I know. Your knowledge in the genre has given me much insight, and for that I appreciate you.

To the many readers who continue to show love and support, I truly thank you with every piece of my heart. Thank you for allowing me to occupy some time in your life, and the opportunity to share a piece of my mind. Without further a due, here is Loyalty 2: Loyalty is everything.

5

LOYALTY II

Chapter 1

"I am the son of Eric Taylor, and you will find out
what that really means!"~ Iras

The loud shrill of the siren practically drowned
out the paramedics' voices in the back of the
ambulance. Iras nervously watched as the medics
tended to Loyal's limp body lying on the stretcher.
The white sheets slowly soaked up her crimson blood
that leaked from the bullet wound on the side of her
head. His legs trembled as his heart beat frantically.
His sweaty hands shook uncontrollably while he
watched them attempt to save Loyal's life. The whole
scene was chaotic, but for Iras, everything moved in
slow motion.

Unable to wrap his mind around what was taking
place, his worst nightmare became his reality in the

blink of an eye. His fiancée and his unborn child were slowly being taken away from him, and he knew there was nothing he could do to save them. Helpless, Iras closed his eyes as warm tears flowed down his cheeks like an open faucet.

This should have been me! he thought. *She didn't deserve this. My daughter didn't deserve this.* Iras gripped his head and rested his elbows on his knees.

"We have a pulse!" a medic shouted as he tried to hold Loyal's arm steady in the moving vehicle. He quickly, but carefully, pierced her skin with the IV needle while another paramedic maneuvered a breathing tube down her throat.

Iras looked up at the medics. They all jerked forward from the ambulance coming to an abrupt halt. Moments later, a gust of air hit Iras's bare arms when the back doors of the ambulance swung open.

"Move. Move. Let's go," one of the paramedics ordered.

As the men pulled Loyal from the vehicle, the legs on the stretcher instantly snapped into place. Iras's bare feet hit the pavement as he followed behind them into the hospital.

"We've got a gunshot wound to the head. She's pregnant!" a paramedic announced after entering through the doors.

Almost simultaneously, every medical personnel stopped what they were doing. The doctors and nurses took control of the situation and pushed the stretcher down a long hallway. One doctor shouted orders to the staff as they passed through the double doors and into a secured area.

"I'm sorry, sir, but you cannot go back there," a young nurse informed Iras, blocking his path.

"They need me!" Iras hysterically replied. "I have to get back there."

"I understand this may be hard for you, but you have to let them do what they need to do to help her."

Iras breathed heavily.

"Sir?" the young nurse called. "Are you okay?" A worried look appeared on her face when she noticed Iras's clammy skin and the deep breaths he took attempting to catch his breath.

"Sir, I think you should sit down," she told him.

Iras didn't respond.

The nurse placed her hand on his shoulder. "Sir?" she said and shook him. "Sir? Sir?"

Iras woke suddenly and shot up in his seat. Sweat beads trickled down his forehead while his heart raced a mile a minute. He looked around at the many passengers staring at him.

"Are you alright, sir?" a woman asked.

Iras looked back and saw the flight attendant standing behind him. He quickly remembered where he was.

"You were shouting in your sleep, sir," the flight attendant continued.

Iras sat back in his seat, took off his all-black Philly's fitted cap, and placed it on the tray in front of him. Since the day Loyal was shot, his mind replayed the same dream over and over...or better yet, the same nightmare.

"I'm fine," he responded to the flight attendant.

A few passengers looked in their direction, then went back to their own engagements.

"Is there anything I can get for you?" she asked.

"Do you have any aspirin?"

She nodded. "Water, too?"

"Yes, please."

"I'll be right back." The flight attendant walked to the back of the airplane.

Iras took a deep breath. He hated the way his mind made him relive that day. He looked across the aisle and locked eyes with a little girl wearing a purple and white dress. On each side of her head, she had two pigtails, which were wrapped in big purple ribbons. She waved at Iras with a huge smile painted on her face.

The little girl's innocence brought thoughts of his seven-month-old daughter, Nijah. He couldn't be thankful enough that God allowed his daughter to survive, that she would grow up and live her life despite her tragic entry into this cold, cold world. The fact that she almost lost her life before she even knew she had one confirmed to Iras that God was real, and his father, Eric, was right next to him looking over his granddaughter. He only wished God would give Loyal another chance. His heart sank at the thought of Nijah never being able to have a normal relationship with her mother or being taught certain things about life that only a mother could teach.

Loyal had survived the shooting. However, her life as she knew it died that night. The bullet that grazed her brain damaged her memory and paralyzed her entire right side. At first, the doctors told him that her condition was permanent. But, after about six months, Loyal began to show signs of improvement. She could move certain fingers on her right hand, and her verbalizations strengthened despite her slurred speech.

Iras hated having to leave them at home in Atlanta, but he knew they were in good hands with Melissa. Melissa was only supposed to be in Atlanta for a short time to help out with Loyal and the baby, but she ended up moving there.

Iras made a vow to always be there for Loyal and their daughter no matter how bad things got. His thoughts instantly switched to his own mother, Monica. The havoc she'd caused in his life was like opening up the gates to hell. He thrashed himself time and time again for even letting everything go down the way it did. He wasn't the full blame, but letting Monica into his life was his contribution to it, and his conscious never let him forget it.

The investigators who handled Loyal's case had no solid evidence of who shot Loyal, but all ten of Iras's fingers pointed to Monica. She had been MIA ever since that night.

"Here you are, sir," the flight attendant said as she approached Iras carrying his requested items.

"Thank you. How much longer before we land?" Iras asked.

"We should be arriving in Philadelphia in about forty minutes," she responded. "If there is anything else I can get you, just press the call button on the overhead panel." The flight attendant smiled before she walked away.

Iras opened the pack of aspirin and popped two small white pills into his mouth. He flushed the pills down with the water and leaned his head back on the headrest.

The day will come when we will meet again, Monica. I am the son of Eric Taylor, and you will find out what that really means!

****

Angel rolled over in her king-sized bed and reached for her husband, Pablo. When she only felt an empty space next to her, she opened her eyes, sat up in the bed, and looked around the room. The soft glow of the moonlight lit the dark room. Angel switched on the lamp sitting next to the bed on the nightstand. The grandfather clock on the wall displayed that it was almost three o'clock in the morning. Angel knew Pablo would never leave her alone in the middle of the night without waking her first.

Assuming he was somewhere in their house, she scooted to the edge of the bed and placed her bare feet on the plush carpet. Just as she was about to stand up, a sharp pain formed in her stomach.

"Mmm," she moaned.

She put her hand on her growing belly and massaged it. She loved feeling her unborn children moving around inside of her, but for the past couple of weeks, the feeling was more painful than anything. Either way, she was grateful to become a mom. At one point in her life, she never thought she would ever love a man enough to marry him or give birth to his child…twins at that. Her father, Mac, planted a seed in her mind a long time ago about men. He was living proof that no man can be trusted. Yet, meeting Pablo was the best thing that ever happened to her. He was the light at the end of long, dark, cold tunnel that gave her a new life.

The pain in her belly eased up enough for Angel to stand. She slipped on her white cotton slippers and headed out of the bedroom. While slowly walking down the long, dimly lit hallway, she held onto the wall to help keep her balance. Just as she approached the top of the stairs, she heard movement coming from Meeka's old room. She walked to the room and saw Pablo through the crack of the slightly open door. She watched as her husband stood at the dresser.

The room was dark, but the light from the night's sky outlined the silhouette of his frame. He held a picture frame in his hand as he stood there, almost frozen. Angel knew exactly what he was looking at. It was a photo of him and Meeka when she was only five years old. Meeka kept the photo on her dresser, and after she died, Pablo kept everything in that room exactly the same. He allowed Angel to remodel their entire domain after they were married. He wanted her to have a space where she could feel like it was hers, but the only room he wanted to stay the same was his deceased daughter's.

A part of his heart turned cold, and as a result, he secluded that part of him from the world after he lost Meeka. Angel hated to see him this way, and the fact that she was part of the reason why Meeka was dead crushed her even more. She wasn't sure how Pablo would take it if she were to tell him everything that happened. So many times she wanted to tell Pablo that her plan was what got Meeka killed. Her love for Pablo ran deep, and the thought of him never loving her again scared her the most. No doubt, Angel was ruthless. Her life's path turned her into a careless soul. She wouldn't hesitate to kill if she needed to, but when it came to Pablo, she was wide open; the only soft spot in the center of the cinderblock that she called her heart.

When she turned to walk back to her bedroom, her hand hit the door accidentally, causing it to slightly creak open. *Damn!* she thought, not wanting to disturb him.

"Can't sleep?" Pablo asked from inside the room. Angel pushed the door completely open and leaned against the doorframe.

"I had to use the bathroom," she lied.

Pablo sat the photo back down on the dresser and walked over to his wife. He gently placed both hands on her cheeks and guided her lips to his. Angel massaged his muscular arms as her body melted into the affection he offered.

"Your arms are freezing," she said after their lips parted.

"I was out on the balcony for a bit," he responded.

He walked back over to Meeka's bed and sat on the edge. Angel flipped the switch on the wall by the door, lighting up the room.

"Sometimes I think she's still away at school," he started. "I know everything about her death is real, but my mind refuses to believe it."

Angel walked over and stood behind him. She placed her hands on his shoulders and gave him a gentle massage as he confided in her.

"She was a good girl. No, she wasn't perfect, but she was my daughter. What did she do to make someone want to brutally murder her?"

A single tear crept from Pablo's eye. He quickly wiped it away and stood from the bed. He walked to the window and looked up at the night's sky.

As usual, Angel remained quiet when he spoke about his daughter. Her guilt ate at her like a plague. Her lips wanted so bad to tell him who killed his daughter, but her heart wasn't ready to confront his reaction when he found out her involvement. She was not ready to accept part of the blame and own up for her dishonesty. Angel knew it was selfish, but for so long, she yearned to be in that happy place, to have the love every woman would kill to have. And now that she had it all, she didn't want to risk losing it.

"I will not stop until I find her killer. These months have passed like minutes, and the longer it takes me, the more pain this city will feel until I do!"

Shivers shot through Angel's body as the words left his lips, knowing he meant every word. Almost a year had passed since Meeka was killed, but Pablo's wounds were still fresh.

"Umm." Angel put both of her hands on her belly and slightly bent over.

Pablo turned around from the sound of her moan. "What's the matter?" he asked, rushing to her aid.

"Just a little pain. It will go away," Angel assured him as she took in deep breaths.

"You should lie down and get some rest. I will have the doctor come by in the morning to check on you."

Angel nodded.

He escorted her back to the bedroom and helped her into bed. He then kneeled down beside the bed so they were face to face.

"I don't know how I would have made it this long if it weren't for you. When God took Meeka from me, he gave me you." Pablo put his hand on her stomach. "And they will never know harm," he said, rubbing his unborn daughters. "I will see to it that nothing ever happens to them or you." Pablo placed a kiss on her stomach, then one on her forehead. "Now rest, my love."

The darkness hid her awkward facial expression as she dealt with her internal battle. Pablo left the room and closed the door behind him.

Fuck, she thought. *How did I let it get this far? I have to tell him. I just hope he's ready to hear it.*

****

"Welcome back," Kino greeted Iras as soon as he walked through the airport doors.

Kino stood up straight from leaning against his black Armada truck and walked over to his boy. His walk had a slight limp from the bullet that pierced his spinal cord when Monica shot him a while back. Luckily for him, a limp walk was all he had sustained from the injury. He slapped hands with Iras.

"You good, my nigga?" Iras asked.

"As good as I'll ever be," Kino responded as he rubbed his goatee. "Let's roll."

Kino maneuvered through the empty Philadelphia streets while puffing on his neatly rolled el. He passed it to Iras as he emptied his lungs of the excess smoke. Iras joined his right-hand man in the cipher.

"Is everything straight for tomorrow?" Iras asked.

"Yeah," Kino answered. "Buttah's home-going service will be just the way he wanted it, family only." Kino's eyes blurred from the tears starting to fill them. "That nigga was a fighter. I really thought he was going to pull through that coma."

Iras nodded as he listened to his best friend. Although Buttah was Iras's godfather, he knew Kino was taking his death harder than him. Kino had a special kind of relationship with Buttah. Iras was fortunate enough to have his father around, but Kino wasn't, and in his own way, Kino looked at Buttah like a father figure. Kino was the one who checked in with the hospital the entire time Buttah was in the coma. Eight long months, Kino made sure to visit Buttah just about every other day and patiently waited for the day he would awake. That day never came. Buttah started bleeding on his brain, and there was no way for the doctors to control it.

"I still can't believe he's gone." Kino shook his head. "Shit has been fucked since ya pops and Buttah ain't around. The work they got out here now is like sugar compared to what we had. That's why we need to link up with ya pops' connect. Plus, this nickel-

and-dime shit is for the birds. Niggas ain't eating right these days, Ras."

"My pops linked up with this new mu'fucka from Jersey before he died, and he only copped from him once," Iras said.

"So reach out to him and see what's good. I mean, his shit must be that work if ya pops started fucking with him."

"He did business with my pops and Buttah; that don't mean we automatically get a pass." Iras blew out a cloud of smoke. "And it damn sure doesn't mean we can trust him. But, like I said before, I'm not getting my hands in that shit right now. I will lose it if something happened to my family again. With that lifestyle, some chances automatically come with it...and I'm not willing to take those chances. The less I'm involved with these streets, the better."

Kino nodded and took the blunt. "I feel you, but I also know who you are. The hustla in you won't let you stay away for too long, and just know this shit ain't going down without you. We been getting money together, and we're gonna keep getting it together. You'll see. Plus, it's too many mu' fuckas in the city fucking it up by making it hot out here for everybody. It's gonna take some real niggas like us to get things back in order."

After their thirty-minute travel from the airport, Kino pulled up to an apartment building on the west side of Philadelphia. There wasn't anything spectacular about the building, and most of the residents that lived there were average, middle-class, working adults and their families. Kino rented out an apartment on the third floor to use as his stash spot. He never drew attention to himself when he stopped there. He always made sure not to carry in any bags, and he left out the exact same way. Kino's money was nowhere near as long as it used to be, but the streets didn't know that. He took every precaution to protect what he did have; there was no such thing as being too careful.

They entered the building and went to the apartment. After unlocking the door, Kino opened it. He immediately froze when he saw two .9mm pistols pointing back at them.

"What the fuck is wrong with you?" a raspy-voiced woman asked from inside.

Iras's first instinct was to reach for his own protection tucked in his waist, but he remembered he wasn't strapped because of the flight he took.

"Damn, Moms, put that shit away," Kino responded.

"Don't anybody just be rolling through here this time in the morning. You better start calling first," she said, then lowered her guns and walked back over to the couch where she had been sleeping.

Kino shook his head as he and Iras entered the apartment and secured the door shut behind them.

"What are you doing here so early anyway? I thought you weren't coming by until this afternoon," Moms said as she flopped down on the couch.

Frances, better known as Moms, was once Kino and Iras's go-to person when they first started hustling in middle school. They were in the eighth grade when they got their first pound of weed from Moms. Even though Iras's dad had his hands in anything that came into the city, they knew Eric would never let them get money that way. Moms even got her wholesale from Eric. She was like the cool old-head on the block. She wasn't big time, and most of the time, she got her fix from her own supply rather than selling it, but she wasn't a stranger to the streets or to the murder game.

When they skipped school, she let them come to her house and do whatever they felt like doing. As long as her money came back straight, she was cool. Moms never had any children of her own, but she called all the young boys in the neighborhood working for her, her children. That's how she got the nickname *Moms*.

She had a special liking for Iras and Kino. They weren't as rowdy as the other boys, and their loyalty to each other and honesty to her was what she loved most about them. She quit her small hustle when diagnosed with type-2 diabetes. Since then, Kino and Iras always had little jobs for her to do to make money. In a way, she had taken care of them, and now it was their way of returning the favor.

"Well, I'll be damned!" Moms said as she lit her cigarette and threw the lighter down on the coffee table. "I haven't seen you in a while. How you been holding up?" she asked Iras, who sat on the loveseat across from her.

"I been a'ight, Moms," he replied. "I had to get away for a little bit. Shit got too crazy."

"Hey, ain't nothing wrong with that." She coughed from the smoke entering her lungs. "Damn!" she said, holding her chest.

"You need some water or something, Moms?" he asked.

She shook her head as she continued to cough. She reached down beside her foot, picked up a cup, and finished drinking whatever was in it. Then she sat it on the table. She cleared her throat before speaking.

"Water ain't gon' help," she joked. "Neither will these damn cigarettes, but fuck it. We all got to die someday. Might as well die happy."

Iras nodded. Moms had been saying that her whole life. It was like her excuse to live on the edge no matter what people may think.

"So, how long are you here for?" she asked.

"Just until the day after tomorrow. My focus is back in Atlanta. I'm only here for Buttah's funeral."

"You know, your father and Buttah were like the saviors to a lot of people when I was coming up." Moms sat back on the couch.

"Yeah," Iras agreed. "They were good people to know, huh?"

26

"Good? They were better than the city's officials," Moms tested. "They kept shit in order. It takes special kind of people to fill their shoes."

Moms nodded as memories of the two filled her thoughts.

"Eric and Buttah," she said in a low tone. "They are really gone." She put her cigarette out in the ashtray beside her. "But, as long as you and Kino are around, their hard work won't go to waste. Knowing y'all, they left the right ones in charge. Just don't let this little break you're on turn permanent. This is your city, and don't you ever forget that."

Iras sat quietly as he took heed to what she said. Part of him yearned to get back into his old life. It wasn't so much the money, but the power. Being the son of a kingpin had its perks, and he always thought about the day when he would step up to the throne. When he would no longer be known as Eric's son, but form his own identity that the street would respect. That day presented itself a lot sooner than what he had expected, and with Loyal and their new addition, he had more to think about when it came to jumping back in. This time around he had a lot more to lose.

Kino stood in the bedroom as he nodded and listened to Moms little pep talk.

If anybody can get this nigga back on track, it's Moms, he thought.

He knew Iras had doubts about getting back into the game after his dad died, so he put Moms up to giving Iras some reassurance, and by Iras's silence, Kino knew it was working.

It's time to take back our city!

Chapter 2

"Trust no one until they prove worthy!"

Three hundred and forty-four days! Monica thought as she lay on her back and counted down to the day of her freedom.

It was the same routine she had day after day at the Cambridge Springs Correctional Institution for Women, which had been her home for the past year.

Three hundred and forty-four fucking days! Your dead bitch. When I get out, you'll wish you were dead when I'm through with you. But, she's your sister; she only did what was right. Well, the bitch should have killed me then! She's the reason why I'm in this hellhole. She's the reason why my son hates me. If it wasn't for her or that whore, Loyal, I would have my son. She will pay for what she's done. They both will!

"Chow time!" the prison guard announced as he walked by her cell, letting the inmates know breakfast was being served. The eight by ten-foot room was more like a crawl space. The steel walls gave off a cold sensation to the room, and there was one solid, barred door that locked from the outside. The sound of the buzzer alerted the inmates that they could open their thick cell doors.

Monica sat up on her bed and looked over at her cellmate, who was tucking pieces of paper under her mattress. The cellmate looked up and caught eyes with Monica.

"Are you going to say good morning or are you just going to stare?" she sarcastically asked.

Monica huffed at the smart remark just as she stood to her feet. She stretched her arms into the air. She still felt the tenderness in her back from being shot by her baby sister, Melissa. Although her wounds healed nicely on the outside, the scars that were embedded inside her still lurked, and she had every intention of ending her sister's life for her betrayal. Melissa was dead to her anyway. Monica had crossed the line with her sister long before Melissa picked up that gun, but in Monica's twisted mind, Melissa was wrong for her decision...and her decision was crystal clear.

Monica walked out of her cell that opened directly to a common area unit. The unit featured ten round silver tables with benches connected to them. She walked up to the front of the unit and stood in the meal line. Her tan shirt and pants blended right in with the rest of the incarcerated women.

After waiting in line, Monica finally got her tray of food and sat at an empty table in the corner of the unit. She shook her head in disgust at the slop they offered them for nourishment, but the only choice she had was to eat it.

Just as she was about to have her meal, another inmate slammed her hands down on the cafeteria table in front of where she sat. Monica briefly stared at the dirty pair of muscular hands. She looked up at the husky inmate and then back down to her food tray. She picked up her plastic fork and resumed her meal, as if the inmate wasn't there.

The inmate slapped the table again, this time pushing Monica's tray to the floor. The clinking of the tray hitting the floor caught a few of the other female inmates' attention. Monica shot her eyes over at the prison guards that stood by the door engaged in their own conversation. She tightened the fork she held in her hand as her patience grew thin.

"I don't like to be ignored," the husky inmate warned her.

Monica slowly rolled her eyes up at her and stared her dead-on. She knew it was only a matter of time before someone in the prison tested her. She'd spent her months staying to herself, and that was just how she planned on finishing her time there.

"I wasn't done eating," Monica replied sternly.

She'd come across some of the grittiest people on the streets, and even when she spent time in her drug rehab, she didn't let anyone treat her like a floor mat. The beastly stature that stood before her wasn't a threat, and by the look she gave her, Monica made sure to get that point across.

"If I didn't know any better, I'd think you were about to stab my hand with that fork," the inmate said, noticing the tightly-gripped utensil in Monica's hand. "But, I know you're not crazy."

Monica smirked. "That's the thing about assumptions." She slowly stood to her feet so she was face to face with the woman. "I will slice...your fucking throat... where you stan—"

The inmate smacked Monica before she could finish her sentence, and she fell to the ground from the impact of the hit. The woman pounced on top of her and beat her senseless. Commotion arose from the other inmates watching the fight. Monica fought back as much as she could, but the weight of her opponent limited her defense. So, she closed her eyes and put up her arms to block the hits directed towards her face. Suddenly, the weight lifted off of her body, and Monica opened her eyes. A few of the other inmates grabbed the woman off her. The woman struggled to get free, but they kept her detained.

"Yo, Big Taz, chill the fuck out," another inmate said.

"Yeah, you better listen to her, Big Taz," Monica mocked and laughed hysterically.

Taz tried to lunge at her but was again stopped by the inmates holding her back. The two women guards that stood at the door quickly approached them.

"I suggest y'all shut the fuck up right now!" one of the guards advised the rest of the ladies on the unit. "Everybody back in their cells, now!" she ordered.

The guards lifted Monica to her feet. She caught eyes with Big Taz. She could tell from the look on Taz's face that it wasn't over.

Come for me if you want to, bitch, Monica thought as she blew a kiss to her. A blown kiss was a signal to let someone know they were on your hit list…kissing your life goodbye.

Taz nodded slowly with her face frowned up.

"I said go to your fucking cells!" the guard shouted again.

The unit cleared as the inmates followed the order they were given. Monica limped back to her cell and sat down on her bunk.

"What the hell did you do to get on Big Taz's bad side?" her cellmate asked.

Monica didn't respond. She lay back on her bed and stared at the ceiling. She licked her lip where she had been hit, and the salty taste let her know she was bleeding.

"See!" her cellmate said. "That's the reason no one fucks with you now. That shitty attitude was bound to get you checked."

"I'm not here to make friends," Monica spat.

"Judging by the way you fight, you *need* to make some."

Monica jumped up from the bed. "Listen, little girl, you don't know me, so don't think you have the right to judge anything I do! Stay in a child's place."

"Quite frankly, honey, I don't care to know you. All I'm saying is that the same rules from out there don't fly while you're in here. You want to walk around here all lonely and stuck up, then you're asking for it."

Monica rolled her eyes. "Yeah? Well, let another bitch try it. They won't be so lucky like that big bitch, and you can tell her I said that."

She flopped back down on her bed, folded her arms, and rapidly tapped her foot as her adrenaline began to decrease. *Who the fuck does she think she is?* she thought.

Her cellmate shook her head. A brief moment of silence passed. A soft chuckle from her cellmate turned into laughter. She lay back on the bed and laughed even harder.

"What the hell is so funny, little girl?" Monica asked, annoyed.

"Your fight reminded me of a movie," she responded. "You ever see that movie *Friday* with Ice Cube?"

"Yeah, but how does the fight remind you of *Friday*?" Monica asked with her face frowned up.

"Because you got knocked the fuck out," she said, still laughing.

Monica frowned. She watched as her cellmate laughed at her expense. Moments later, Monica couldn't help the tickled feeling in her stomach and began laughing herself.

"It's not that damn funny, okay."

"You had to see the way you were fighting from the ground," she joked.

"She snuck me, and for her sake, she should be glad she did!" Monica scooted back on her bed and leaned her back against the wall. "It's Terria, right?"

"You've been my cellmate all this time and you don't know my name? Girl, your street smarts are shittier than I thought," she said, shaking her head. "But, no. It's Theresa."

Monica sucked her teeth. "Same thing," she joked.

"Yeah, whatever," she said. "You better take heed to what I've told you."

Monica nodded. It was the first time she had an actual conversation with Theresa. Even though she didn't plan on getting to know any of the ladies there, the last thing she wanted was to have to sleep with both eyes open.

I might as well make the best of this situation, she thought. *I could use this little bitch until I'm done with her.*

"Oh, and Monica?" Theresa called.

Monica looked over at her.

"Don't think just because we spoke today that we're friends," she told her. "You got to earn your stripes around here like everyone else."

Monica dismissed the thought of even trying to fit in as fast as Theresa suggested it.

Yeah, I'll earn mine alright! she thought.

Theresa didn't know that Monica danced to the tune of her own agenda. Monica knew exactly what she was doing, and Theresa had been unknowingly added to the game.

****

Iras pulled into the Embassy Suites on 17th and Vine in an all-black Dodge Charger. It was Kino's back-up car that he drove while he was in town. He pressed the button on the keypad and set the car alarm before he walked through the sliding glass doors.

He had just come from viewing his godfather, Buttah, for the very last time. He didn't plan on attending the burial ceremony. It was hard enough seeing Buttah in the casket. He didn't want to have the visual of the casket being lowered into the ground. Buttah looked as if he was in a peaceful sleep, and Iras was content with that.

Iras never foresaw the day would come that both his father and godfather would be just a memory. They were like the Martin and Malcolm of the streets, and the dynasty they created was supposed to be untouchable. Iras still couldn't figure out how the once most notorious men in the city got caught slipping. He knew his father wasn't a predictable man, especially when it came to the streets. That right there told him one thing: someone on the inside caused Eric and Buttah's deaths. They never kept too many soldiers around them, but the ones that were around quickly jumped ship once they learned their leader died. They didn't even bother to show up to Buttah's funeral.

Iras walked up to the front desk where an elderly Latino woman stood speaking to a scrawny white boy.

"If you come in late again, that's it!" she said as Iras approached. She then turned her attention to Iras. "Welcome to the Embassy Suites," she greeted with a smile. "How can I help you?"

Iras looked at the boy as he walked to the back with his head lowered. "Checking in, please," Iras affably responded.

"Do you have a reservation?"

"Yes, Mike Carter."

"Mr. Carter, I will need credit card and ID please."

Iras casually pulled out a neatly-wrapped stack of one hundred dollar bills and placed them on the counter. The woman frowned up her eyebrows in confusion.

"I would like a room on the top floor," Iras said. "Just for the night. A thousand should cover it."

The woman paused, nervousness written all over her face. She stared at the stack of bills, and Iras knew she was trying to fight the temptation of taking the amount of money she would have had to work double overtime to make. The woman looked around before sliding the money off of the counter. She briefly finished checking him in and handed him a key card.

"Suite 1530."

Iras grabbed the key card and headed up to his room.

He opened the door to the two-bedroom suite, walked in, and tossed the key card on the coffee table. He toured the entire suite, but not because of the fancy trimmings and upscale settings. He toured the suite to make sure he was alone. In the past, he had learned the hard way because of his mistakes, and his paranoia kicked in whenever he was in an unfamiliar place. He tried to leave as little room for error as possible.

Iras walked over to the full-length mirror in the master bedroom. Standing in front of the mirror, he adjusted his tie. He sported a black Dolce & Gabbana wool suit with a pleated, all-white button-up shirt. Iras wasn't the suit wearing type. In fact, it was the first time he put one on since his father's funeral. He was comfortable just rocking a pair of designer jeans and tops, but the more he stared in the mirror, the more the GQ look appealed to him.

The reflection he stared at in the mirror resembled his father. Iras nodded in approval of the man he had become. He had left the streets alone, something he knew his father always wanted him to do, but the urge he had for the power still lied deep inside of him. The conversation with Moms unleashed that urge like a wild lion. He was ready...ready to continue the Taylor legacy. Iras was a natural born hustler at heart, but watching his father, he picked up on what he needed to do to be a boss. He knew it wasn't going to be an easy task because he had been out for so long, and every move he made had to be strategic.

If I'm going to do this, I'll have to go undetected, he thought, while looking intently at himself in the mirror. *No one needs to know that I'm back. It's going to be too many wanna-be hustlas bringing unnecessary heat my way if they know Eric Taylor's legacy is back.* Iras put the master plan together in his head. *Moves must be made in silence and two steps ahead of everyone else.* He rubbed his chin as he mentally prepared himself for what was to come. *And last but not least, trust no one until they prove worthy.*

Iras pulled out his iPhone and swiped his thumb across the screen searching through his contact list. He tapped the call button when he came to Melissa's number and briefly waited for the call to connect.

"Hey, Ras," Melissa answered.

"What's good?" he replied, sitting down on the bed. "How's everything?"

"Everything is good. We just got in from visiting Loyal at the hospital."

"How is she holding up?"

"My girl is a fighter," Melissa assured him. "She had therapy today, and they tried to get her to walk. She still doesn't remember a lot, but she knows who we are and she's hanging in there. And little Ms. Nijah is sound asleep."

"Yo, Melissa, thanks for everything," he said with sincerity. "I've got a few things to handle here, but I will be making my way back as soon as I'm done."

"You don't have to thank me, Iras. We're family."

"Yeah, but I don't know how the fuck I would've kept pushing if it weren't for you," he told her. "And even though Loyal ain't in her regular state of mind, I know she appreciates it."

"It's all good," she assured him. "But, Ras, I got to call you right back. That's the hospital beeping in on the other line."

"A'ight, go and get that. Let me know what's up." Iras ended the call and put his phone back into his pocket.

He jumped up from the bed when he heard someone knocking at the door. He pulled the .357 Magnum he'd got from Kino from his waistline. No one knew he was there, especially since he checked into the room under a fake name.

Iras eased to the door with his gun, ready to pop off. He looked through the peephole and saw the white boy that was at the check-in desk. He let out a sigh. *Get ya'self together, nigga!* he thought as he tucked his gun away and opened the door.

"Welcome to the Embassy, sir," the boy said. "My name is Danny, and I'm just checking to make sure everything is okay with your suite." The boy had to be no older than nineteen. He had dark-brown stringy hair and brown freckles covering his cheeks.

"Yeah, man, everything is cool," Iras said, looking him up and down. He noticed the pair of worn-out black Air Force Ones he was wearing, along with the stains on his uniform. "Your boss wouldn't cut you a break down there, huh?"

Danny didn't respond. Iras could tell by the look on his face that he felt uneasy.

"I heard her getting on you when I came in."

"I've been late a few times," Danny replied.

"Well, take it from me. Late and money don't mix."

"Yeah, I know." Danny nodded. "But, I can't leave for work until my dad gets home to watch my little brother. I can't just leave him alone. It's just us, and I'm doing the best I can to play my part."

Iras didn't expect him to go into that much detail, but by the way he was so open with it, Iras sensed the boy just needed to vent...a feeling he knew all too well.

"But, I'll be okay," Danny continued. "She says that all the time, but the most she's ever done was write me up."

Iras nodded. Something about Danny made him feel a bit of sympathy.

"Okay, sir. Well, if you need anything, just dial forty-four on your room phone," Danny said as he walked away.

"Yo, Danny?" Iras called out. "You'll be here all night?"

"Just until eleven tonight," he responded.

Iras pulled out a wad of money, peeled off a single hundred-dollar bill, and held it out. Iras saw Danny's eyes light up at the sight of it.

"Oh, sir, tips are not necessary. We..."

"It's not a tip," Iras said, cutting him off. "I need you to call this room if anybody else checks in on this floor tonight. I need you to keep it between you and me. Can you do that?"

The boy nonchalantly shrugged. "Sure, why not?" He took the money and slid it into his back pocket before walking away.

Iras didn't care who was checking in on his floor. It was his way of getting Danny to accept the money. It was his way of helping out the young kid, knowing he probably needed the money. His father, Eric, always told him that situations are presented to people for specific reasons...find the reason and you'll find your purpose. It was meant for him to help Danny, and he didn't think twice about it.

As the hours passed, the night began to cover the sky. Iras reached out to one of his dad's old goons, Black. He needed a way to get in touch with the coke connect from Jersey, and Black was the only one who would know how to reach him. He called him once, but got no answer. Iras wasn't fond of blowing up someone's phone, because he felt if they wanted to call him back, they would. One missed call was all it took to get someone's attention. So, he waited anxiously for Black to return his call. Moments later, he received a text message from Black's number. He opened the text, but it was empty.

He replied to the text. *Yo, Black, it's Ras.* After a few minutes, Iras's phone rang. He quickly answered it when he saw it was Black.

"Yo."

"My fault, Ras," Black responded. "I just had to make sure it was really you. Is everything okay?"

"I need a favor," Iras told him. "Is there somewhere we can meet?"

"This must be serious," Black responded. "We can meet, but I'm in New York now. A lot has changed, and I rarely come to the city nowadays. I wanted to come to Buttah's funeral today, but shit is just too complicated right now. If you want to meet, it will have to be in a couple of days."

"We can come to you," Iras replied.

"We?"

"Me and Kino. We can be there tomorrow."

Silence grew on the phone. Iras sensed the awkward feeling.

"Black, it's important."

"Okay. I'll text you an address in the morning," Black told him. "Just you and Kino," he said before hanging up.

What the fuck was that all about? Iras thought as he looked at his phone. He shook his head and dismissed the thoughts.

New York was on his agenda for the next day, and if all things went according to plan, major changes were in the near future.

Chapter 3

"Kill her! Kill her before she kills you!"

Monica sat on the prison's yard soaking up the sunrays beaming down on her. They weren't let out in the yard very often, so when they were, she made sure to appreciate it. It wasn't the same as being in the real world, but after being behind those funky walls for so long, the fresh air was like a breath of heaven. High gates with barbed wire at the top surrounded the yard. Guards were stationed in high towers just in case someone got brave enough to try anything.

Monica watched as various inmates engaged in their own activity. In a way, the prison reminded her of high school. Cliques formed in different areas of the yard and each person knew their boundary. She spotted Theresa on the bleachers waving for her to come over.

What does that bitch want now? she thought.

Monica stood up and walked past the groups of inmates. She locked eyes with Big Taz, who was sitting on a weight bench at the far end of the yard. It had been three days since their encounter, but Monica knew their beef was far from over. Eventually, she was going to have to cook it. Her eyes stayed on Taz as she approached Theresa.

"Come kick it with us," Theresa offered.

Monica scanned her eyes across the group of girls that Theresa sat with, and they returned the glare.

"This is Cash, Sara, and Ronnie," Theresa introduced, while pointing to each person.

"Monica," she stated with a blank stare as she introduced herself. She felt as though all eyes were on her—because they were. She sensed Taz was still grilling her, and when she turned around, her suspicion was right on point. Taz's eyes were glued. Monica smirked at her, knowing it would piss her off.

Theresa turned her head to see what Monica was staring at. "You two haven't made up yet?" Theresa asked jokingly.

"I'm not worried about her," Monica assured her. "If she really wanted me, she would have been handled it."

"Yo, T!" another inmate shouted from across the yard.

Theresa looked in the direction of the person calling her name.

"Come here for a sec."

Theresa nodded her head. "I'll be right back," she told them before walking off, leaving Monica with her crew.

"So what's your deal?" Sara asked with her heavy southern accent, looking up at Monica. She squinted her eyes from the bright sunlight.

You ain't ever hear of a dentist? Monica thought when Sara exposed her encrusted grill. Her teeth were poorly rotten, but it was the perfect fit for her trailer-trash appearance. Her dirty-blonde, stringy hair was tied back into a messy ponytail, and her pale skin must have taken on an age of its own. Monica knew her type all too well and could tell she had her share of heroin in her lifetime.

"Shit happens, you know? I just go where life takes me. Just so happens, I ended up here," Monica answered. She wasn't about to let anyone know her reason for being there...as if it were any their business anyway.

"Ha!" Sara chuckled. "So you're one of those types, huh? Innocent until proven guilty. Well, look-a here, honey. Just about every lady up in here is innocent, if you let them tell it."

"I never said I was innocent," Monica responded, "and if you..."

"What the fuck is going on with that?" Cash said, jumping up from her seat.

Monica turned to see what had her attention. Theresa stood in front of Big Taz. From their body language, the conversation looked intense.

"Are they friends?" Monica asked out loud as she watched the two.

"Big Taz isn't friends with anybody," Cash replied.

Cash, Ronnie, and Sara stood to walk over, but Theresa put her hand up, signaling for them not to come over. Monica just watched the entire ordeal. Theresa frowned at Monica briefly before finishing up whatever she and Taz were talking about.

Make friends, my ass! Monica thought. *This bitch is trying to set me up! She must not know who she's fucking with? I got you, bitch! But, you don't even know what she's talking to her about! I saw the way see looked at me. That bitch is foul.*

The voices in Monica's head rattled up her fury and persuaded her to think that Theresa was against her.

"File in!" a prison guard shouted.

Their outdoor recreational hour had come to an end. Monica retired to her cell and lay on the bed.

I have to get rid of her, Monica's thoughts continued. *I have to get out of this place.*

She looked up when she heard Theresa coming into the cell. A guard stood on the other side of the door and momentarily watched them through the rectangular window. Theresa waited for the guard to walk away. When the coast was clear, she tossed a homemade weapon onto Monica's bed. Monica looked at the contraption and then up at Theresa.

"I swiped that from Big Taz," Theresa gloated. "I was in the middle of talking to Deena when I saw her ass coming towards you. I stopped her because I knew what she was about to do. The last thing we need around here is to be on lockdown. She would have fucked it up for all of us."

"Humph." Monica sat up on the bed. "So she just *let* you keep it?"

"She probably thinks it's still in her pocket."

Or she probably gave it to you for you to use on me! Monica thought.

Ignoring the fact that Theresa had possibly just saved her life, in Monica's twisted mind, Theresa couldn't be trusted.

"And what reason do you have for doing that?" Monica asked. "You don't know me, but you're so quick to jump into something that doesn't involve you."

"First of all, I didn't just do it for you," Theresa snapped back. "And you can put your stank-ass attitude back in its place because I don't have time for that shit. I did it because I was just like you when I first came to this place. Bitches were out to get me because they didn't know who I was. If it weren't for my old cellmate, Angel, I probably would be dead right now. You should learn to appreciate when someone shows you loyalty around here."

Monica's heart fluttered when she heard the name Angel...a name she hadn't heard in a long time. An image of her best friend flashed through her mind. The Angel she mentioned couldn't possibly be her friend, Angel. She knew Angel had been locked up for most of her life, but what were the odds that Monica ended up with her old cellmate?

"But, you know what?" Theresa flopped down on her bed. "Next time, I'll just mind my own damn business." Theresa folded her arms across her chest. "But it ain't like Angel's ass knows what loyalty is her damn self," she huffed to herself.

Theresa laid back on her bed.

Still consumed in her thoughts about Angel, Monica stared into space. Angel was the only one who Monica could be herself around—good or bad. They were as different as night and day, but blood couldn't make them any closer. Their life's choices separated them when they were only teenagers. Angel went to prison, but destiny drew the paths leading them back to one another. When they reunited at Eric's funeral, it was like Monica's life was coming back together. She had her friend back, and it was like nothing had changed between them.

Curiosity evolved inside her, and Monica wanted to know more. She quickly switched her attitude to appear a little more concerned. Manipulation was definitely one of her stronger assets.

"Listen, Theresa, it's not that I don't appreciate it. It's just that I feel like I'm going crazy in here. All of the shit I see going down in here...I don't know *who* I can trust," Monica said sincerely.

"And you may never know, but just know that if you're down with me, then I'm down with you. I was raised to be a woman of my word, and my word is the only thing I have left."

Monica nodded as if she believed her. She waited for a brief moment and then asked, "What happened with your old cellmate? Angel, right? I heard you say she wasn't loyal either."

Theresa shook her head. "It's nothing. I mean, it's my fault for thinking I could trust her once she left this place. She was doing me a huge favor, and in return, I had my uncle, Pablo, out in Jersey set her up with a place to stay until she got back on her feet."

Oh my God! Monica's eyes widened. *That can't be possible.* She remembered Angel telling her about her new man, Pablo, and how she was in love with him.

"I mean, it was cool for the first couple of months, but all of a sudden, the letters stopped coming," Theresa added. "When I tried to call, the number was changed. Uncle P didn't even reach out to me."

"Wow," Monica said. "Did she ever do what you asked her to do?"

Theresa shrugged. "I can't tell you if they're dead or alive. But, that's one fucked up bitch. It's disloyal bitches like her that won't last long out there anyway."

Hearing Theresa talk about Angel that way triggered her defense. She wasn't one hundred percent sure if her Angel was the one she was referring to, but just thinking about it was enough. Theresa had crossed the line when she cursed Angel's name.

"Only to you," Monica said in a devilish tone.

"What?" Theresa heard the evident change in her tone. "What's that supposed to mean?"

Monica slowly stood to her feet and grabbed the homemade weapon from off of her bed.

"You're just as grimy as the next bitch. Don't sit here acting like your shit doesn't stink," Monica said as she slowly walked toward her. The malice in her voice was like the devil himself had awakened.

"Monica, what the fuck are you talking about?" Theresa stood up when she noticed Monica holding the weapon.

Kill her! Kill her before she kills you! The voices in Monica's head fed her adrenaline; it pumped and pumped. Her harried heartbeat made her chest feel like it was ready to explode. The only time she got that feeling was when she saw blood, and at that point, it was no stopping her. Images of Theresa and Taz flashed through her mind.

Monica walked until she was face to face with her and held the sharp end of the weapon towards her. Theresa saw the deranged look in Monica's eyes, but it wasn't enough for Theresa to back down.

"You crazy bitch," Theresa said. "What the fuck do you think…"

Monica turned the weapon on herself and rammed it into her own abdomen. She cringed slightly from the brutal piercing.

"What the fuck!" Theresa shouted, shocked at what she just witnessed.

Monica removed the weapon and stabbed herself several more times. Her hands were covered in blood. Then she lunged her bloody body at Theresa. Blood was everywhere, even on Theresa's hands and clothes. Theresa jumped on her bed, and Monica's body dropped to the floor just as she let out a scream.

Theresa's eyes bulged out of her head. She stood on the bed frozen, while Monica continued to scream. Several guards burst into the cell from the uproar.

"What did you do?" one of the male guards yelled.

"She…she," Monica tried to muster up her words, but her body felt too weak to even breathe.

Two of the guards grabbed Theresa off the bed and dragged her out of the cell.

"She's fucking crazy!" Theresa screamed. "She did it to herself!"

The guards ignored her as they restrained her.

"You have to believe me!" she pleaded.

"Then how did you get her blood on you?" a woman guard sarcastically asked.

Theresa struggled and pleaded with the guards while trying to explain what happened, but it was no use. Her pleas fell on deaf ears.

****

Three days had passed since Iras and Kino took their mini-trip to New York to meet with Black; a trip that gave them what they needed to regain the streets. Black set it up for them to meet with a man by the name of Mr. Gomez. Kino hit the Atlantic City expressway, with Iras riding passenger, and followed the directions they were given. The sun began to set and gave off a fiery tint in the sky. The cool summer breeze felt perfect after a blazing day.

"Yo, we need to hit up the tables while we're out here," Kino loudly said. "I'm feeling lucky."

Iras reached for the volume knob on the radio and turned it down. "You'll fuck around and lose all your money, knowing you," Iras joked. "But, it's whatever after this meeting."

"Of course. Business first," Kino responded. He looked in the rearview mirror to make sure it was okay for him to switch lanes. He turned on his left signal and glided into the left lane. When he glimpsed back in the mirror, he noticed a white truck a few cars back merging into the same lane. Normally, he wouldn't have paid it any mind, but he peeped it was the same truck that had been behind him since they left Philly. Kino reduced his speed, letting the other cars pass him.

"The way you're driving we might not make the meeting," Iras joked. "Why the hell are you driving so slow?"

Kino didn't respond. He looked in his mirror again and saw the truck was still behind him even after he slowed down. He merged to the far right lane, and just as he suspected, so did the truck. Kino got off at the next exit, which were two exits earlier than the exit they were supposed to get off.

"Kino, we don't have time for any pit stops," Iras said. "Why are we getting off here?"

"I want to see something," Kino responded. "Look behind us."

Iras could tell something wasn't right. He turned his head and looked out the back of the truck. The only thing he saw was a white Cadillac Escalade getting off the exit, too.

"That truck has been behind us since we left," Kino told him. "I didn't think too much of it at first, but these mu'fuckas is definitely following us."

Iras pulled his steel piece from his waistline and held it in his lap. Kino pulled into the first gas station he saw when he got off the expressway. He stopped at the gas pump but left the engine running. He watched as the truck pulled into the gas station and up to another pump.

"Who the fuck is that?" he said. He didn't know anyone with that kind of truck, and the tinted windows made it impossible for him to look inside.

"Well, there's only one way to find out," Iras said.

Just as Iras touched the door handle, two women got out of the truck and walked into the gas station. Kino stared to get a good look, but he had never seen those women a day in his life. Iras looked back at Kino and shook his head. He shut his door and put his gun away as he laughed to himself.

"Let's go before we're late."

The Atlantic City lights lit up the night. AC was like a mini Las Vegas minus the showgirls. All the local hustlers went there and put on a show by betting large amounts of money, trying to out bet one another. It was also a set up to see who was really bringing in the stacks, and more than likely, their ego would stir up a war.

Iras and Kino walked into the grand lobby of Caesar's Palace. Just as instructed, they took the escalator up to the casino floor. Iras scanned the loud establishment. *Bingo!* he thought. He spotted a man standing at the bar wearing an all-white designer suit and white shoes to match. His jet-black hair was slicked back like one of those hoodlums in the old mobster movies. *That must be him.* Iras approached the bar with Kino following behind him.

"Tango?" Iras asked.

"Are you alone?" the man replied with his Spanish accent, never looking their way.

Iras looked at Kino and back to him. "Yeah, it's just us."

"Follow me."

He led them up to the top floor of the forty-three-story building where another suited man stood in front of one of the rooms.

"Have they been searched?" the man asked Tango as they approached.

"You don't have to search us," Iras interrupted.

He pulled out his strap and held it out. Black had already put him down to how Mr. Gomez rolled, and he knew giving up his piece was one of the conditions. Kino surrendered his gun, as well. Tango took both pistols, but still patted them down before leading them into the suite. If it were any other situation, Iras would have been insulted about still being searched after willingly handing over his gun, but he understood the precautions.

"Wait here," Tango instructed them, then disappeared into another room.

The suite was huge and spectacular but nothing that was foreign to them. They stayed at some of the best hotels and resorts across the country.

"You've made it," a man said as he entered the living room. "Please, have a seat." He took a seat on the single chair and motioned for them to join him.

Iras and Kino took seats on the leather sectional.

"Mr. Gomez?" Iras asked.

"Please, call me Pablo," he suggested. "Cigar?" Pablo opened a wooden box that sat in the middle of the coffee table, exposing a row of Ashton ESG Cigars.

Iras declined his offer. Pablo took one of the cigars and the stainless steel cigar cutter and clipped one end off of the cigar. "So, I hear you're trying to continue your family business. That's some pretty hefty shoes to fill."

"I was taught well," Iras responded.

"You know, your father was a good man. I didn't know him long, but from the time that I did, I could tell." Pablo took a puff of his cigar. "But, his partner I'm not so sure about—Buttah, is it?"

Iras nodded.

"What part would he play in this if I decide to extend an offer?"

Iras paused. He didn't know what gripe he had with a deceased man, but he knew it wasn't his place to ask. "He was laid to rest a couple of days ago."

"I see." Pablo blew out a cloud of smoke. "Do you know good cocaine when you see it?"

Pablo snapped his fingers and Tango brought over a neatly wrapped brick of the powdered treat.

"This right here is the purest you will find." He pulled out a pocketknife and made a single small cut, just enough for Iras to sample.

Iras rubbed a small amount on his gums and almost instantly he could feel it going numb.

"Damn," Iras said in a low tone. It had been a while since he last tested coke, but nothing he had in the past compared to what he just experienced.

Kino took his sample and nodded at Iras.

"Now my question to you is, how much can you handle?" Pablo continued. "Am I to expect that you will be as good of a customer that your father was?"

"That depends on what they are going for." Iras sat back on the sectional. "For right now, I'm looking to only grab a few, but if the price is right, you can expect that reoccurring order. Feel me?"

Pablo put his cigar out in the ashtray. "Because I liked your father, I'll let it go for fifteen each."

Iras's eyes widened in disbelief. Fifteen thousand a key was a deal of a lifetime, especially because hard times had hit the streets and no one got a brick for that price.

"Just let me know how many and I'll have Tango deliver them in a few days."

"No doubt!" Iras said, extending his hand.

Pablo grabbed his hand as a sign of a sealed deal. Then he got up from his chair and walked over to the mini-bar.

"Mr. Pablo?" Iras called. "Just out of curiosity, are you always this loose with people?"

"What do you mean?"

"You took our guns, but nothing else. You didn't check for wires or nothing. Why do you trust so easily?"

"From the moment Black called and told me about you, I had eyes on you. The most beautiful pairs of eyes you will ever see. So beautiful you wouldn't even notice them watching you." Pablo responded with a wink. "Now come, let's have a drink."

Iras instantly thought of the white truck. He looked at Kino and could tell they were thinking the same thing.

LOYALTY II

Chapter 4

"The first time I wrapped my lips around it, it was the sweetest thing I had ever tasted."

Angel hovered over her bathroom sink while the cold water ran down the drain. She hoped quenching her thirst would soothe the pain she endured in her stomach. It didn't work. She took deep breaths as she tried to control the pain. It was the worst pain she had felt thus far during her pregnancy. The only thing she could think of is that her body had to be going into labor. With eight weeks to go, the thought of delivering early was horrific. Sweat beads trickled down her face as her breathing got heavier. Since the last time she experienced pain, Pablo hired a midwife to look in after her, but that night, she gave her the day off thinking it would be okay. She regretted her decision. She knew Pablo wasn't going to be home for a few more hours, so she was on her own.

I have to get to the phone, she thought.

Her body felt extremely weak, but she knew she had no other choice but to go back to her bedroom. Angel held on to the wall as she took each dreadful footstep. The pain seemed to grow worse by the second. She felt moisture developing between her legs and trickling down to her bare feet. Halfway down the hall, she dropped to her knees in agonizing pain and tightened her legs with her hands between them.

"Oh God!" she screamed. When she removed her hands, they were covered in blood. *Please, God, let my babies be alright.*

The worst thoughts traveled through her mind as she gathered what little energy she had left and scooted the rest of the way to her bedroom. A trail of blood followed behind her. Feeble and distraught, she managed to make it to her phone. The room was spinning and her fatigue was uncontrollable. She dialed 911 and waited for an answer, but finally, everything went black.

****

The sound of the hospital machines faded into Monica's ears. She slowly opened her eyes, and the first thing she saw was a large white board with the date on it. She looked around and immediately knew she was no longer in the prison. She felt lightheaded and groggy, but she was pleased to be anywhere besides there. She spotted the guard sitting in a chair asleep with his hat over his face. She thought about what she did, and the last thing she remembered was Theresa being taken away. A wicked smile spread across her face. She needed a plan to get out of the prison, and it actually worked.

She moved her leg and felt something restraining her ankle. She tugged on the sheet that covered her to expose her feet. *Fuck!* Monica thought. Her ankles were connected to the bed with metal chains. *I've got to get out of here.*

The door opened and a woman walked in wearing a white doctor's coat. Her attention was focused on the clipboard she was reading, so she hadn't noticed Monica was awake.

"Excuse me?" Monica said.

"Oh!" the woman jumped. "You startled me." She walked to the top of the bed and extended her hand. "I'm Dr. Bryant. I'll be the floor resident for tonight."

Monica shook her hand.

"How are you feeling?" she asked as she pulled the sheet down and lifted Monica's hospital gown to check her injury.

"I'll live," Monica replied nonchalantly.

"Well, you were stabbed pretty deep. You had to undergo a minor surgery in order for us to control the bleeding." She looked at Monica's stomach. Her incisions were covered with clear medical tape. "I just have to make sure it doesn't get infected, but you're right. You will live." She smiled as she covered her back up. "Press the call button if you need anything. You may feel tenderness, but you shouldn't feel any pain. If so, I can give you some morphine. Are you allergic?"

Monica shook her head.

"Perfect," Dr. Bryant said before she left out of the room.

The guard woke from the door closing. Monica stared him down briefly.

"Nice of you to finally wake up," Monica sarcastically said. "Do you always sleep on the job?"

The guard cut his eyes at her.

"Oh, I see you're not the friendly type. Listen, the only company I've had in a while is a bunch of funky bitches, so excuse me for wanting a change in scenery."

"Hush," the guard ordered. "We are not friends. You're a prisoner, so stay in your place."

If this were any other situation, you would be dead talking to me like that, she thought.

She stared at him almost as if she was studying him. His boyish features didn't look a day older than twenty-five. He was medium built with a light skin complexion, almost as light as her. Monica knew he was new to the job. It wasn't hard to sniff out a new prison guard; how long it would take to break them in was the question. It was no secret that some of the male guards were having sex with inmates. Monica never did and never had planned to, but in this situation, she was going to make an exception.

He is going to be my way out of here whether he likes it or not.

"You like this job?" Monica asked, changing her tone. "I mean, you can't possibly be here for the money, because I know they ain't paying shit." She waited for an answer, but he didn't respond. "I couldn't do it," she continued as if they were having a mutual conversation. "Knowing me, I would have been caught up. I don't know how you can control yourself. Isn't it tempting?"

"What?" he finally answered, cutting his eyes over at her.

Gotcha, Monica thought. "Being around so many women...the easy access, you know. I know you heard how it goes down in Cambridge," she said, smiling.

"I don't get into all of that," he replied. "Besides, most of them bitches are nasty anyway."

"Not all of us," Monica said, trying to keep the conversation going. "Not the ones I had a piece of," she lied.

The guard shook his head. "You better be careful who you're fucking with in there. You'll wind up with that shit you can't get rid of. Everybody ain't real about they shit."

"Are you?" Monica asked seductively.

The guard looked her in the eyes. "I'm always real about mine," he said, adjusting himself in the chair. "So you're into women, huh?"

Monica smiled. *This is going to be a breeze.* "I wasn't until I was sent to prison. Ain't too many options, so a bitch got to do what she got to do."

"It's easy for a woman. Ain't no way in hell I'd be fagging it out if I was locked up." He chuckled. "I love pussy too much."

"I didn't think I would love it as much as I do. The first time I wrapped my lips around it, it was the sweetest thing I ever tasted. I was all the way turned on. Don't get me wrong, I love me some good dick, but this feeling was different. It was gentle, and she knew every spot to make my body yearn."

As the lies flowed from her lips, Monica knew she had peaked his interest. She noticed the bulge that appeared through his fitted uniform pants. She licked her lips seductively.

The knocking at the door interrupted the conversation.

"Good evening," a short, heavyset white woman announced as she entered the room pushing a tan cart. "I'm Margret, the unit's RN. I just need to get a few blood samples for the labs."

Monica nodded. The nurse began working on Monica's arm.

"I need to use the bathroom," Monica told her.

The nurse looked at the guard for his approval.

"Damn, I can't pee!" Monica blurted out.

"Uh, of course. I'm just following procedures. He has to make that decision," the nurse nervously responded.

"Well, I guess he can clean the shit up, too, if I just go right here in this bed," Monica sarcastically replied.

She hated being treated like a prisoner from the guards, even though she was, but it burned her up even more to be treated like one from a nurse.

"I said I have to use the bathroom."

"It's okay," the guard finally said.

The nurse quickly finished collecting Monica's blood and disconnected her from the machines. The guard got up from the chair and walked over to the bed.

"Hold out your arms," he instructed as he pulled out a pair of handcuffs.

"How am I supposed to use the bathroom with those on?"

"It's procedure," he responded. "I have to free your ankles from the bed, so you have to put these on."

"You can leave now," Monica told the nurse who was watching as the guard put the cuffs on her wrists.

"I was waiting to see if you need any assistance, but if you're good…" The nurse shrugged. "Give me a shout when she's finished so I can hook her back up to the monitors," she told the guard before exiting and shutting the door behind her.

"You're tough." The guard smirked.

"I'm not really. I just hate when people don't give me the respect I deserve."

"Yeah, but can you blame her?" the guard asked as he removed the ankle restraints.

"Yes," Monica sternly said. "Just because I'm in jail doesn't mean I'm lower than she is. Everybody is one crime away from being locked up their damn selves, especially those white people. They snap at the drop of a dime."

They shared a laugh.

"C'mon," the guard said, extending his arm.

Monica grabbed his arm and slowly eased off of the bed. She felt a great deal of pressure in her abdomen as she stood to her feet. The guard carefully escorted her to the bathroom a few feet away. Pain crept in with each step Monica took. She didn't have to pee, but it was the only way for her to be disconnected from the hospital monitors. What she had planned would have definitely set them off.

The guard stopped when they reached the bathroom, but Monica pulled him inside.

"Do you need help going, too?" he sarcastically asked.

"I think I do," Monica said as she maneuvered her body in front of him. Her hands found their way to his manhood and gently massaged it through his pants.

"Yo, ma, you got to chill with that right now," he said.

"He doesn't think so," Monica responded, referring to his stiff shaft. She stared him in the eyes as she unbuttoned his pants and pulled out his dick. By now, he was at full attention.

"This isn't right, ma," he said. He could have easily stopped her, but didn't.

Monica held on to him as she eased down on her knees.

Oh my God! A piercing pain shot through her body like a lightning bolt. She kept her face lowered so he wouldn't notice her excruciating facial expression and bit her bottom lip to keep from screaming.

You have to do this; it may be your only chance. She took in a deep breath and looked back up at him just before taking the tip of his penis inside of her mouth. Watching him, she circled her tongue around the head. Then she slowly slid her mouth deeper down on him, making it touch the back of her mouth.

"Damn," he moaned. He reached for the bathroom door and closed it.

Monica began to bob her head slowly, as he watched his dick disappear in and out of her mouth. Grabbing his dick with both of her hands, she began stroking his shaft. It had been a long time since Monica gave a man head, but she worked him as if she hadn't lost a beat. Her head game was something serious, and by the guard's reaction, she was putting in work.

He leaned up against the wall for stability. His legs trembled, and his dick was the hardest it had ever been. He gently grabbed her ponytail and moved his hips to the same motion as her head. She removed her lips from him.

"You like that?" she asked, stroking him with her hands.

Without waiting for him to respond, she devoured him in her mouth one again.

Monica felt her kitten purring between her legs. She slid one hand down to her peach and massaged it gently. Knowing that she could be caught any minute was turning her on even more. Her body feed off of the thrill of it.

She lay down on the cold, tiled bathroom floor. She pulled up her hospital gown, exposing her glistening pussy. Her hands glided back down to her kitten and she initiated her own self-pleasure. The guard stood over her, stroking his dick as he watched her fingers squirming around and around.

"Oh, shit! Mmm," Monica moaned, playing into the tease. Her stomach throbbed so badly that she couldn't enjoy the pleasure from her fingers.

The guard joined her on the floor and buried his face in her vagina. He was rough and sloppy, and Monica knew from his ways that he had never pleased a woman orally. Monica pretended to enjoy it as she rubbed her fingers through his sandy brown hair. She caressed his temples and then his ears. He briefly paused when the chain from the handcuffs got in his way. He pulled the chain downward, and it slid perfectly under his chin. The guard continued with his amateur techniques.

"That's it," Monica said in a low tone. "Right there."

She slowly crossed her wrists behind his head so the chain from the handcuffs was close around his neck. The chain wasn't very long, but just long enough for the perfect fit. She took deep breaths as she gathered every ounce of strength she had left.

One...Two...Three! Monica held her hands together and forcefully pulled upward so the chain cut the guard's airways. His eyes widened when he realized what was happening. He tried to grab the chain from around his neck, but he couldn't get a grip on it. Monica pulled it tighter and tighter. The guard fought back, throwing blows to her stomach.

Monica tried her hardest to hold back her screams. He was hitting her so hard that it felt like her wounds were opening back up, but she refused to let go. She held on as his body squirmed like a fish needing water. When Monica noticed him reaching for his gun attached to his pants, she quickly wrapped her legs around him to control his hands. His light skin had turned to a flushed red tint as his air supply became thinner and thinner. She yanked harder and harder—so hard that the handcuffs began to dig in her own wrist. The guard's punches weakened and his fight started to give in. Their eyes locked and Monica felt no remorse for what she was doing. It was as if she enjoyed the look of fear in his eyes. As his squirming slowed down, Monica knew his fight was coming to an end. She held on until his body briefly stiffened right before collapsing on top of her.

Breathing heavily, Monica slowly loosened her grip, making sure he was dead. She collapsed on the floor as she tried to slow down her breathing. After a brief moment of recouping, Monica rolled the guard's dead body off of her. She searched him and found the key to the handcuffs. Monica freed her wrists and scooted herself over to the bathroom sink.

Holding on to the sink, she pulled herself to her feet. She stared at herself in the mirror, something she hadn't done in a long time. She touched her face in almost disbelief that she was in her real skin. The bags under her eyes made her appear weary. Once a woman who used her looks to get a pass in life, she was now staring at someone who had grown accustomed to hurt and pain. Her face showed it all.

Monica looked down at her stomach and saw that her hospital gown was stained with blood. She slid off the gown and tied it tightly around her stomach, applying pressure to stop her wounds from bleeding.

"I've got to get the hell out of here," she said to herself. She looked down at the corpse lying on the floor. "And you're going to be my way out!"

LOYALTY II

Chapter 5

"What happened to Meeka is the past and I will not make him re-live it."

Monica cracked open her room door and scoped out the scene on the other side. It was normal. A few nurses sat in front of computers in the nurse's station located in the middle of the floor. Monica shut the door and leaned up against it. She looked straight ahead at her blurred reflection in the large wall-sized window. She looked back down at herself and adjusted the guard's jacket that she was wearing. She had clothed herself in his entire uniform and made sure all of her hair was tucked into the hat.

Monica opened the door again and walked out of the room with her head lowered. Despite the pain she was feeling, she tried to remain as straight as possible while walking past the nurse's station and heading towards the elevator. She pressed the button to call the elevator. *C'mon.* She turned to look back at her room and saw the nurse in front of her door looking over her chart.

Oh shit! Monica began to panic. She pressed the button again, but still no elevator. She looked back and saw the nurse grabbing the doorknob.

Alarms sounded throughout the floor and several nurses, including hers, immediately ran to the problem. The elevator door opened and Monica stepped on. Relieved, she leaned up against the wall and headed down to the main entrance.

I don't know what just happened, but I'm glad it did.

She got off the elevator and walked right out the revolving front doors.

The city streets were alive. A mixture of different music from the cars played and pedestrians walked along the sidewalks. The streetlights lit up the night and the smell of food from nearby food stores filled her nostrils. Monica took in every last sensation that she had been missing since being sent to prison. She slowly walked to the corner of the block where there was one of the hospital's several parking lots. This parking lot was small and only held about fifty cars opposed to the other parking garages. She slowly limped past the parking lot and a white woman standing at her car talking on a cell phone.

"Excuse me, officer," the woman called.

Monica continued walking.

"You're...leaking something," the woman said as she squinted her eyes trying to see what it was.

Monica stopped in her tracks. She looked back and saw traces of blood.

"Are you alright?" the woman asked, concerned. "James, I'll call you back," the woman said into the phone and closed it shut.

"I'm... I'm hurt," Monica replied. "I need help." She hunched over and grabbed her stomach. "Ahh," Monica moaned as she discreetly grabbed the gun on her waistline. She had taken it from the guard knowing it was much needed.

The woman rushed to her side, and in one swift motion, Monica pulled out the gun and put it to the woman's side. She stood close to her so she wouldn't draw too much attention to herself. The people who did bypass them were distracted with their own conversations with each other.

"Oh my God." The woman grew petrified. "I don't have any money," she pleaded.

"But you have a car," Monica said sternly. "You try anything and I will fill your insides up with this lead."

The woman nervously nodded.

"Walk," Monica ordered.

The woman frantically unlocked her car and got into the driver's seat. Monica got in the backseat directly behind her.

"Are you going to kill me?" the woman asked, frightened.

"Do exactly what I say and I won't have to," Monica warned her. "Give me your cell phone and drive."

"Where to?"

"Just drive," Monica said.

The woman did as she was told. She drove around for twenty minutes with no real destination. Monica sat in the backseat contemplating her next move. She didn't want to kill her, but she knew the woman would cause more problems for her if she let her live. The roads got darker and there were fewer streetlights where they were.

"Pull over right here," Monica ordered.

The woman slowly brought the car to stop and switched the gear to park.

"Take off your clothes."

"What?"

"Do it or I'll blow your fucking brains out," Monica threatened.

The woman began to cry as she took off her purple cardigan and floral-printed sundress. "I'll do whatever you want. Just please, don't kill me," the woman pleaded.

"Pop the trunk and get out."

The woman did as she was told, and Monica got out with the gun pointing at her. She looked around; they were the only souls on the dark road.

"Get in." Monica nodded towards the trunk.

The woman looked at the trunk and back at Monica. "Please don't do this."

Monica cocked the gun and gritted her teeth.. "Now!"

The woman climbed into the trunk wearing nothing but her panties and bra, and Monica slammed it shut. Then she hurried into the driver's seat and pulled off. She drove around for about ten minutes in a town she knew nothing about. She finally saw a gas station and pulled into it. Entering the gas station, Monica immediately scanned the place. An Arabic man sat behind the counter watching a small black and white television.

"Excuse me," Monica said. "Where is your bathroom?'

The man slid a large metal ring with a key attached to it across the counter. "Around the back."

Monica took the key and left out. The bathroom wasn't as dirty as she expected it to be. She removed the guard's clothes and placed them on the floor so her feet wouldn't be directly touching the dirty floor. She turned on the water and grabbed a hand full of paper towels from its dispenser. She needed to clean the blood off of her body before changing into the woman's clothes.

She cleaned up as much as she could. Her wounds had stopped bleeding, but she still felt like shit. She put on the dress and cardigan and slipped into the woman's sandals. Almost the perfect fit, Monica was pleased with her *new* get up. She didn't bother returning the bathroom key; she just needed to get far away from there.

She got back into the car, and spotting the woman's purse on the floor, she searched through it. She found the woman's driver's license, family photos, and cash—four hundred dollars to be exact. The woman also had several bottles of medication. One was a bottle of Vicodin. She opened the top, popped a pill, and swallowed them without anything to drink. She reached to the backseat for the woman's cell phone. She loaded up the GPS and typed in Iras's old address. It was five and a half hours from where she was, but that was her next stop.

"Mommy's coming!" she said in a malicious tone, then put the car in gear and drove off into the night.

****

Angel slowly opened her eyes. *Where am I?* Feeling something pressing against her face, she reached up to grab it. She felt her face, and there was a tube taped to it leading into her nose. She saw the IV in her hand and the machines she was hooked up to. She heard her heart beating in her ears as she tried to remember what happened.

A hospital? What happened? She gasped. *Oh no, my babies.* She felt her stomach and discovered she was no longer pregnant. *Oh my God! What happened? What happened to my babies?*

Tears flowed down her face as she thought the worst. She remembered her doctor telling her it was going to be difficult for her to carry because of the three miscarriages and two abortions she had in the past. The times when she didn't know she was pregnant, she was still working under Mac's supervision. The abuse and sexual escapades caused her to miscarry, and the abortions...well, she was damned if she was going to have a child by her own father. No matter how much Angel tried to leave the past behind her, it had a way of sneaking up. It was as if Mac had cast a dark shadow over her life. His actions years ago were the cause of the pain she was currently indulging.

Pablo entered the room and a smile brushed across his face.

Angel looked toward the door. "You're here," she said, feeling a bit relieved.

He walked over to her bedside. "Of course, I am. Where else would I be?" He bent over and gently kissed her on the forehead. "How are you feeling, my love?"

"The babies," she cried. "What happened?"

"They're fine," he assured her. "You had to have an emergency C-section. I'm glad the police found you when they did. I thought I almost lost you and our daughters."

"Where are my girls? I want to see them."

"They are in the intensive care unit. They will have to stay in the incubator until their lungs are strong enough."

"Oh my God," Angel sobbed. "This is all my fault."

Pablo held her hand. "They are strong. They have my blood running through them, which means they're fighters. You did well. Don't blame yourself."

Angel closed her eyes as she held onto Pablo's hand. "I love you," she whispered.

"I love you, too. More than you may know." Pablo kissed her once more. "Thank you for giving me life again. Now rest. You need it."

Angel's warm tears were not enough to soothe her cold conscious. *I won't hurt him,* she thought. *He doesn't deserve to be hurt again. What happened to Meeka is the past, and I will not make him relive it.*

That very moment she decided to bury her decision to tell Pablo the truth and never bring it to mind again.

It's time for us to just be happy.

Chapter 6

Ain't nobody fresher than my clique!

Trina stretched her body across her king-sized bed in her Lower Marian brownstone. It had been almost a year since Corey convinced her to move back to the east coast. Even though Buttah was dead and Corey guaranteed her that she had nothing to worry about, she couldn't shake the bad feelings that often crept up in her stomach. In Atlanta, she felt safe, like God was giving her a fresh start at a new life with Corey and her godson, Akahi. Philadelphia was where she had buried all of her demons, and now that she was back in that mental graveyard, she felt as if karma wasn't too far away.

Trina rolled over onto her back and stared at her ceiling fan spinning.

"Are you sleeping?" a tiny voice asked.

Trina lifted up onto her elbows and saw Akahi standing at her door.

Smiling, she said, "Yes, I am."

"No, you're not." Akahi laughed. "Your eyes are still open."

Trina laughed, too. His seven-year-old innocence always seemed to brighten up the room. She sat completely up on the bed.

"Come here," she said, holding out her hands.

Akahi ran over and jumped on her bed and into her lap.

"You know, you're starting to look more like your mother every day," she told him.

"Nu uh," Akahi said. "Mommy said I'm becoming a handsome young boy."

"Oh, she did, huh?" Trina asked. "And when did she tell you this?"

"When I pray to God, he lets me talk to her." Akahi smiled.

Trina's emotions began to surface and her eyes watered up. "Well, the next time you speak with her, you tell her I said hi. Okay?" Trina kissed him on his forehead. "Now go put your shoes on. I have a surprise for you."

Akahi's eyes lit up and he ran out of the room to do what he was told. Trina released a sigh as a few tears fell down her face. Akahi's mother, Keilani, had been dead over a year, but she still wasn't ready to let her go. Visuals of the night Buttah killed Keilani haunted her.

It should have been me, she thought. *I should have died in the car that night.*

Trina wiped her tears away and reached for her cell phone. She dialed Corey's number only to receive his voicemail.

"Hey, babe," she said into the phone. "I was just letting you know that I'm taking Akahi to Keilani's gravesite today. Then we're going to grab a bite to eat. Maybe you can meet us for lunch. Give me a call. Love you."

Trina threw her phone on the bed and got up to prepare for her day.

As Corey walked out of the post office, he pulled his cell phone away from his ear to look at the screen when he heard someone beeping in. He saw Trina's name flashing on the screen and sent it to voicemail.

"I need you to make sure everything is straight before I leave for the islands," he said into the phone. "I don't want to be getting any calls about shit fucking up. I'm counting on you to handle this while I'm gone, Silas." He continued his conversation as he approached his car. "A'ight, meet me at the spot tonight around seven. One."

Corey ended the call before getting into his car. He opened up a manila package that he had just retrieved from his P.O. Box, a long awaited package that came just in time for the vacation he had planned for him and Trina. He slipped his hand into the box and pulled out a small, red velvet ring box. He opened it and studied the pink 34-karat, Princess-cut, diamond engagement ring that he had custom made. He planned the entire vacation for the very purpose of proposing to her.

Corey never had any intentions on settling down until Trina came back into his life. She wasn't like any of the other women he dated. With her, he could be as open as the sky. Trina knew all about the things he associated with, and it was one of the things that drew him closer to her. When Corey got wind of the infamous Eric Taylor, he knew getting Buttah out of the way would be to his benefit. He already had things on lock in Atlanta, but he saw the opportunity to triple his money by moving back to the east coast. Therefore, he brought his troops to Philly and took over all the trap houses Eric and Buttah once ran. He jumped in so fast that there wasn't time for any of the other hustlers to make a move…and even if they did, he quickly shut them down.

Corey closed the ring box and slipped it into his glove compartment. He pulled out of the post office's parking lot. He didn't want to call Trina back just yet because he had a few more things to handle to add to his surprise before heading home, and he knew she would want to know what he was doing.

I'm going to make her the happiest woman in the world, he thought. *She deserves it.*

****

Silas bumped the hit single "Clique" by Big Sean in his 2012 Grand Marquis. The sun beamed through his sunroof and sweat moistened his body. It was one of the hottest Friday afternoons, and he was en route to collect from one of the trap houses oversaw in south Philly.

He wanted to make sure everything was on point so Corey wouldn't have anything to say. It was the first time he would be running things, and this was his chance for him to prove himself. Silas had been working with Corey for three years...from Atlanta to Philly. He was one of the loyal soldiers, and he always felt Corey knew it. Why else would he have brought him to the east coast? At twenty-three, Silas knew the importance of a man's word, and he made it a point to always keep his.

He pulled up to the corner property where two young hustlers, Khalil and Wayne, sat on the front stoop. He sprung out of his car, leaving the engine idling.

"What'chu think, you LL or some shit?" Khalil yelled out.

The two guys laughed as Silas approached them.

"Ha! Fuck you, lil' nigga. It's hot as a bitch out here," Silas said as he slapped hands with them. "And you could, too, if you start hitting the gym. Bitches don't like no scrawny nigga," he commented, flexing one of his arms.

Silas sported a dark blue tank top that showed off his huge cut arms, with a pair of black Dickie Capri shorts and black Timberland boots. He was caramel brown skin with a dark low haircut and had dimples in his checks. His grey eyes added the finishing touch. Some people considered him a pretty boy, but he was as *hood* as they came. He didn't mind getting his hands dirty if he needed to.

"How's it looking?" he asked. "Everything good out here?"

"Shit, man, it's been slow all week," Khalil said.

"Slow?"

"Yeah, ain't too much poppin' out here today. It's like a ghost town," Khalil told him. "We're still sitting on what you gave us on Tuesday."

Silas frowned. "What the fuck? Niggas ain't getting high no more?"

"I don't know." Khalil shrugged. "We out here, though," he said with a sly tone.

Silas cut his eyes over to Khalil. "Don't start with your bullshit today," Silas warned him.

"I'm just saying." Khalil shook his head. "If I wanted to be on the block, I could have just stayed back in the A. When are we going to talk about that promotion?"

Silas shook his head. "When the time is right. Besides, Corey is running the show. I'm just executing it."

"Well, being as though you two are close now, you need to holla at him," Khalil responded. "You and I both know I can put in that work."

Silas nodded. He knew Khalil was right, but he also knew Corey had no intentions on making him anything more than a pusher. Silas and Khalil were both two peas in the same pod; they made money pushing dope out of one of Corey's trap houses in Atlanta.

They had been friends since kids, but were completely different. Silas was more low-key. Even though he hustled, he still attended school and got good grades. He even finished a bachelors' program at Clark Atlanta University and got a degree in business. He considered his hustle to be smart, and eventually, he would make enough money to start his own record label. Khalil, on the other hand, was flashy and always had to have the latest of everything. He barely made it through high school. Not because he didn't know the work, but because he felt like it was a waste of time. Making money outweighed anything to him. That was one thing Corey didn't like about Khalil. Silas had to convince Corey to even bring Khalil to the east coast. A lot of people didn't understand it, but that was his friend and he wasn't going without him.

Silas nodded. "A'ight, I'll holla at him," he told Khalil, knowing Khalil was never going to drop the issue until he agreed. "Keep holding it down out here." Silas slapped hands with them again. "I'll get back with y'all later."

He got back into his car and pulled off.

Iras and Kino sat in the truck a few doors down from Silas's trap house. They did their homework on him. If they were going to put their plan into motion, they had to find out who was moving all the work in the city. They kept a close eye on Silas, but by the way he moved, they came to the conclusion that someone else was heading the operation... and it was about time for them to find out who it was.

Kino got out of the truck and walked down the block to where Khalil and Wayne sat.

"What's up?" Kino asked as he approached them.

Khalil stood to his feet. "We good, fam," he defensively replied.

Kino put his hands up. "Whoa, this is a friendly visit," he declared when he saw the tension building.

"I don't know you, fam." Khalil shook his head.

"Yeah, I know," Kino said, rubbing his goatee. "Your boy Silas does, though. Let him know his *new boss*, Kino, stopped by."

Khalil frowned up his face. "What the fuck are you talking about?"

"You'll find out soon enough." Kino folded his arms across his chest and tucked his hands in his armpits. "I'll be back here in a few days. Tell your boy we need to meet." Kino was slightly cocky, but he knew his impression was going to stick. "A'ight, Khalil?"

"How the fuck you know my name?"

Kino winked. "Good day, gentlemen," he said before he walked back to his car and got in.

He looked over at Iras and said, "He got the message," then pulled out of the parking space.

Iras nodded. "We need to head downtown to meet up with that mu'fucka, Tango."

"Are you good going alone?" Kino asked. "I need to handle something. It's personal."

"I'll be cool," Iras assured him. "Just drop me off at my car."

****

Trina sat on the grass in front of the black-plated tombstone carved into the shape of a teardrop. The tombstone featured a photo of Keilani with a pink breast cancer ribbon flowing around the photo. The words *I am my sister's keeper* were engraved into the plate. Trina had it specially made for her shortly after Keilani died.

Keilani didn't have a proper burial because the police couldn't find any family she had. The only way they were able to identify her was because of the pink dog tag she wore around her neck with her information on it. That's what the morgue told Trina once she tracked Keilani's body down. She felt bad that she wasn't there to give Keilani the homegoing service she deserved, but she knew if she had stayed, she would have been dead or in jail.

Trina watched as Akahi placed the last few white roses in front of his mother's monument and then sat back on Trina's lap. She hugged him and placed a kiss on his forehead. Her eyes were flooded with tears, but they were hidden behind a pair of dark-tinted Christian Dior sunglasses.

"You know your mom loved you very much, right?" Trina asked in almost a whisper.

"I know," Akahi responded softly. His head was lowered into his chest.

Trina lifted his chin with her hand to make him look at her. Her heart skipped a beat when she saw the tears moving down his face. She hated the fact that Akahi was old enough to remember because of the pain he was feeling, while at the same time grateful that his mother's memory would always be with him.

"And no matter what happens, I will never let you forget her," Trina said. "Even if you start to forget things about her, I will help you remember. Okay?" She pulled him back to her and held him tightly. "I love you, Akahi."

"I love you, too, Auntie Trina."

"Come on," she said as she stood him up. "Let's go eat."

Trina got up from the ground and dusted off her denim shorts.

She held Akahi's hand as they walked back to the parking lot of the cemetery. When she saw a familiar face getting out of the truck parked next to her car, she stopped in her tracks. Her heartbeat sped up as she locked eyes with Kino. The last time she saw him was at Buttah's house just before she took the money. As far as Kino was concerned, Trina was Buttah's woman. Buttah wore her like a trophy for the world to see.

Breathe, she told herself. *He may not know.* She pressed the unlock button on her keypad and put Akahi in the backseat.

"Long time," Kino said as he approached her.

"Hey," she responded. "Yeah, it has been a while."

"Where have you been?" he asked. "You didn't come to the hospital; I didn't see you at the funeral; I—"

"I didn't think it was appropriate for me to come," she lied, cutting him off.

"Trina, you were his woman," Kino said. "Why wouldn't it be?"

Trina shifted her weight from one foot to another. "Listen, Buttah and I…things just didn't work out. Okay?" She walked past him to the driver's side. "I got to go," she said, then got in the car, started the ignition, and pulled out of the parking lot.

He doesn't know! Buttah didn't tell him. He would have killed me if he did. Her thoughts consumed her mind as she drove far away from Kino. A horn blasting scared her from her thoughts.

"Ahh!" She panicked and slammed her foot on the brakes, bringing her car to a screeching stop. "Oh my God!" She looked in the backseat. "Are you, alright?" she asked Akahi.

She had been so busy thinking that she rolled right through a stop sign and almost hit another car.

Akahi nodded. Trina put her hand over her chest and got herself together. *Change of plans. We're going home,* she thought.

Kino walked through the cemetery as he looked for Buttah's plot. He was just there a week ago when Buttah was lowered into the ground, but he felt the need to get something off his chest, and the person he always confided in was Buttah. He didn't think any more of seeing Trina; he just figured she was there to visit Buttah since she didn't come to the funeral. Finding Buttah's plot, he stood over it.

"I promised you that I would visit as much as I can," he said. "Still fucks me up how fast shit can change. I mean...if I would have known when you dropped me off that day it would be the last time we spoke, I would have told you how I really felt. I was waiting until you woke up from the coma to tell you to your face, but..." Kino paused as a tear slid down his face. "You and Eric taught me and Ras a lot," he continued. "You've made men. And I want to thank you for showing me how to be a man, because until I meet Ras and y'all, I didn't have that. I don't know how I would have turned out." Kino wiped the tears from his eyes. "I love you, man, and I promise...I promise if you show me who did this to you, I'll make sure it's handled."

Kino leaned over and kissed Buttah's tombstone before returning to his car.

Chapter 7

"If he shows his face around there again, handle that nigga!"

The sound of a man tapping on the car window woke Monica from her sleep. After driving all night to Philadelphia, she was beat. When she arrived at the condominium where Iras lived, she parked on a side street next to the building. She had a good view of his living room window to watch for any movement in the condo, but sleep crept in and she could no longer fight it. She cracked her window and stared at the man.

"Are you okay?" the man asked. "I saw you here when I left out for work this morning, and I was shocked to see you still here. I wasn't sure if you were dead or not."

Monica grabbed the cell phone and looked at the time. It was almost five-thirty in the afternoon. She slept through the entire day.

"Yes, I'm fine," she told the man before rolling the window up.

Monica put her hand on her forehead. "Oh, God," she moaned.

Her skin was sticky from the heat that generated inside the car as a result of how hot it was outside. Luckily for her, she was parked under a tree that blocked the sun from beaming directly on the car. She felt bleary, and the pain in her stomach felt as if she had gone ten rounds with Mike Tyson. Monica grabbed her stomach trying to ease the pain. The pain wasn't as bad as the night before, but it was still putting up a good fight. She dug through the woman's purse and pulled out the bottle of Vicodin. She popped another pill to help her cope with the pain.

She counted the windows on the building until she got to Iras's window. The building was exactly how she remembered it. The only thing different was the sign hanging on the fifteen-story building that read *Under New Management.* The concierge stood at the entrance door, along with the valet, awaiting the guests.

She watched for hours as darkness finally filled the summer sky, but there had been no movement in her son's place. Monica pulled down the visor, flipped open the mirror, and assessed her face under the dim mirror lights. She undid her ponytail, letting her hair fall down to her shoulders. She then pulled out a make-up kit that she found in the woman's pocketbook. She applied the cosmetics to her face as best as she could to temporarily hide her imperfection. She needed to look as normal as possible, especially since the police had probably blasted her picture all over the news. The only lipstick the woman had was a bright pink; it didn't really fit her, but she made it work. Monica ran her fingers through her hair once more, closed the visor, grabbed the woman's pocketbook, and got out of the car.

Oh shit! Monica thought when she remembered that the owner of the car was still in the trunk. The woman hadn't kicked or screamed, so there was no way of telling if she was still alive. Monica walked to the back of the car and slid the key into the trunk's keyhole. She looked around before turning the key and lifting the trunk just enough for her to peek in. Monica gasped as she let the trunk swing fully open.

This can't be! she thought while staring at the empty trunk. *Fuck! I should have just killed that bitch when I had the chance. She's going to cause more trouble than I need right now.*

Monica had no idea when or even how the woman escaped from the inside of the trunk, but at that point, she didn't have time to worry about that. Monica slammed the trunk closed and walked across the street. She kept her head turned away from the valet as she walked through the front entrance. She quickly scanned the small lobby and focused her attention on a young girl sitting behind the front desk. The girl looked her way when she entered the building.

"Mrs. Taylor?" the girl blurted out as Monica approached the desk.

Taylor wasn't Monica's real last name, but it was what the girl had called her since Iras introduced her to Monica. "Oh my goodness! How have you been? How is Iras?"

Shit! Monica thought. She didn't expect to run into any familiar faces.

"You know him," Monica responded. "Just as wild as he wants to be." She laughed through the lie that flowed from her mouth.

The girl leaned on the desk and shook her head. "I would have thought a baby would have calmed him down."

A fake smile was painted on her face as thoughts of Loyal having her grandchild sent chills through her body.

"So are y'all moving back?" the girl asked. "I was wondering why y'all would just leave the condo empty after it's been paid up in advance."

"Child, I've been telling him to get rid of this condo for months," Monica lied. "But, he wanted to keep it just in case I needed it."

"He is truly one of a kind." She smiled. "Well, welcome back." The girl stood up straight from the counter. "Oh, wait a minute." The girl disappeared into the back and returned with a brown box. "Can you let Iras know his mail is really piling up? I spoke to him when he first moved to Atlanta and he gave me the address to have it forwarded, but they still sent it here. He will need to contact the post office to forward it himself."

Atlanta? Monica thought. *I didn't expect them to still live here, but damn.*

"Oh wow, that's a lot of mail," Monica stated. "I don't know why the change of address didn't go through." She began searching through the top few pieces of mail. "What address did he give you?"

The girl turned the box around and showed Monica the address written on it. Monica read the address, making sure she memorized it.

"Oh, there's the problem," she said. "The address is one-two-four not one-three-four. But, don't worry. I'll take care of it." Monica smiled. "I have to grab my bags from the car. I'll be right back," she said, before heading toward the door. She repeated the address over and over again in her head to make sure she didn't forget it.

She walked out the front door and froze when she saw the red and blue flashing lights and the swarm of police at the car she had stolen. Her heart felt as if it had fallen into the pit of her stomach.

"May I help you, ma'am?" a male voice asked.

She looked up at the doorman standing next to her and then focused her attention back at the police action taking place. While inside the building, she hadn't even heard the sirens. Yet, the police were all over the vehicle.

Monica looked around nervously and spotted a cab parked at the end of the valet.

"I need a cab," she finally responded.

The doorman started to speak, but Monica walked off before he could offer his assistance. She approached the cab and got into the backseat.

"I need to get to the train station," she instructed.

A middle-aged Italian man turned around to view his passenger. "No problem, sweetie," he said with an unlit cigar dangling from his mouth. He tossed the newspaper that he had been reading on the seat next to him and started his engine.

Just as the cab driver pulled off, Monica saw some of the police officers heading over to the building.

"Looks like there's some action going on," the cab driver commented. "You'd be surprised at all the crazy things that happen in the best neighborhoods."

"Oh, I can imagine," she said in a low tone, then rested her head back on the headrest. *I know it was that bitch that sent the police there. Why didn't you just kill her? Damn, Monica, you stupid fuck!*

She cursed at herself for not cleaning up her tracks. It was a good thing she was heading for Atlanta, because by her being on the run, she knew she would have to get as far away from there as possible. Her time as a free woman would more than likely come to an end eventually, but as long as she got to all of the people on her shit list, the ride would be well worth it.

****

Khalil stood on the stoop in his usual spot. He had been out there all day and was ready to call it a night. He pulled out his cell phone and dialed Silas's number again. The call went straight to voicemail. He had planned on telling Silas about the visitor that had stopped by earlier that day, but Silas hadn't answered any of his calls since he left.

"A'ight, fam," Khalil said to Wayne. "I'm out. I got a couple of things to handle in the morning, but I'll be out here when I'm done."

Wayne nodded and Khalil walked off, hopping into a squatter car that Silas bought for him when he moved to the east coast. The car wasn't much to brag about, and it definitely wasn't anything he was used to driving. Silas told him to tone it down because they were moving to an unfamiliar city; the less attention the better. The car served its purpose. He got to wherever he needed to go and back, but back in ATL, he was pushing something more fitting for a man. He worked and saved to buy an all-black Jeep with the rims to match. Khalil was never the type to wait for anyone to give him a handout, but the way he was being handled made him feel less than a man. He left behind friends and family to chase paper he barely saw. Silas told him that this was going to be a power move, but Khalil had yet to reap any of the benefits. He really felt he had been doing better down south and contemplated going back.

Khalil pulled up to his studio apartment in the heart of north Philadelphia just as his phone began to vibrate. He looked at the bright screen.

"Oh, now this nigga wants to call back," he said when he saw Silas's name. Khalil tapped the speaker button. "Yo."

"What'chu mean yo?" Silas snapped. "You're supposed to be on your job. Where you at? Money ain't going to make itself."

"What?" Khalil responded.

"I'm out here; Wayne is out here, but you ain't," Silas rumbled. "Something's wrong with that picture."

Khalil looked at his phone in disbelief that Silas was speaking to him in such a disrespectful tongue. "Yo, Silas, chill the fuck out with all that," Khalil stated with discontentment.

He had no idea why Silas was coming off the way he did, but whatever the reason, Khalil didn't feel the need for him to be talked down to. Silas knew better than anyone that Khalil was far from soft, and had it been any other nigga talking to him that way, Khalil would have made sure they weren't able to say another word.

"Naw, fam, you know how it goes," Silas responded through the muffled phone speaker. "You need to hit me up whenever you leave your post."

"I've been hitting you up all day," Khalil defended. "I'll be at my spot if you need to get at me." Khalil hung up the phone, unwilling to listen to Silas's rampage.

He got out of his car and went inside to his first floor studio apartment. *That nigga on something foul right now,* he thought as he locked the door behind him and flicked on the light switch by the front door.

His studio apartment was only big enough for him. The open space featured a full-sized bed, a sofa, and a black card table with two folding chairs to match. Two doors sat in the far corner of the room, one leading to the bathroom and the other hid the closet space.

Khalil took off his New York Yankees fitted cap and tossed it on his dresser. He sat on the side of his bed and emptied out one of his pants pockets, placing the contents into the top drawer of a nightstand by his bed. He pulled off the blue and white POLO shirt that he wore, exposing the Glock .40 tucked in the waistline of his jeans, and took off his butter-tan Timberland boots. He placed them neatly together by the wall where he had several pairs of shoes lined up. He reached into the other pocket and pulled out a wad of money wrapped in a red rubber band. A majority of the bills were ones and fives. He counted out his take for the day and separated it from the money he had to give to Silas. Out of the nine hundred he had collected, only three hundred was his to claim.

"This shit is a waste of time," he said.

The feeling of regret for even coming to Philly was sinking in more and more each day. He was ready to go back to his hometown where he knew he could get into a better position.

Khalil jumped at someone banging on his door. He jostled over to the single window by the door, peaked through the cheap white blinds, and saw Silas's car sitting in the middle of the street. He grabbed the money he counted from off the bed and opened the front door.

"What the hell is wrong with you hanging up on me like that?" Silas said as soon as he saw Khalil's face.

Khalil's nostrils were instantly ambushed by the smell of alcohol emitting from Silas. He could tell Silas was drunk. He looked at Silas's car and saw two women waiting.

So that's why this nigga is playing that tough role, Khalil thought. *Showing off for these bitches.*

Silas had one weakness...women. Ever since they were teenagers, Silas did the unthinkable to impress a woman. They were like a drug to him, and he was more than willing to fulfill that high. That weakness was intensified when he added alcohol to the picture. There was a time in his life where he couldn't get Silas to even look at a drink. Now it had become a regular weekend routine for him.

"Here," Khalil said, putting the money in Silas's hand.

Silas looked down at the money and a smile grew across his face. "Now that's what I'm talking about." Silas removed the rubber band and counted the money.

Khalil stood in the doorway with his arms folded across his chest and a disgusted look on his face. He thought about putting Silas in his place about the way he was acting, but past experiences told him that he would be wasting his time. But, he was definitely going to make sure he got it off his chest when Silas started thinking straight again.

Silas finished counting the bills and stuffed them into his pocket. "Listen," he said with his eyes low. "You know how you been talking 'bout that promotion, right?" Silas tapped him on the arm. "I got the perfect job for you, fam. While Corey is out of town, I'm running shit. So, I want you to handle things at the South Philly and West Philly spots. Make sure shit is running smooth there, and I'll let Corey know you were the one handling everything. Once he sees you can handle it, he won't have a problem putting you on his front line."

"Yeah, we'll see," Khalil nonchalantly responded. "But, yo, some nigga named Kino came through the spot today talking that shit."

"Kino who?"

Khalil shrugged his shoulders. "He talking 'bout he's your new boss or some shit. He supposed to come back on Monday, and he said he expects to see you there. This mu'fucka even knew my name. He wasn't on no beef shit, though, but he was cocky."

Silas shook his head. "I don't know 'em, so he can keep expecting all he wants to. If he shows his face around there again, handle that nigga." Silas turned to walk away and paused. "On second thought, that nigga might be the feds or something. We ain't got shit for him," Silas said, before walking back to his car.

Khalil stood and watched as Silas drove off. He wasn't sure what was going on, but his mind was already set. By this time next month, he would be back in Atlanta making his own money.

LOYALTY II

Chapter 8

"...I'm going to wake up and this will all be over."

Trina opened the sliding glass door that led directly to the private beach. Her foot sank into the warm sand as her blue sheer wrap danced around her body from the light breeze. It was her first time going to Jamaica and never had she imagined a more beautiful place. The sun had begun to set, casting the perfect red tint in the sky, and the ocean stretched as far as the eye could see. She inhaled deeply, taking in the refreshing, clean air Jamaica had to offer. She walked closer toward the rumbling ocean just enough so the water tickled the edges of her feet.

She was a long way from home, and after running into Kino at the cemetery, the change of scenery was exactly what she needed. She wanted so badly to just be at peace. Ever since she moved back to Philly, she had been more cautious than ever, but the feeling that something bad was about to happen lingered in the pit of her stomach. Seeing Kino made it ten times worse.

"What's on your mind?"

Startled, Trina turned and saw Corey standing behind her enjoying the view of the ocean.

"You scared me," she said. "I didn't even hear you come out."

"I got you, ma," he said as he walked up to her and slid his arms around her tiny waist. "As long as I'm breathing, you ain't got shit to worry about."

"You know I'm going to hold you to that, right?" she said, melting into his arms.

He placed a kissed on the side of her neck.

"Thank you," he whispered into her ear.

"For what?"

"For everything." He put his cheek against hers. "For making me become a better man. Before you came into my life, I didn't have any reason to care, to love, or to feel. My life was missing something, and it wasn't until you appeared that I knew exactly what that was."

His words were like music to her ears. She loved the way he wasn't shy about expressing his feelings to her. It made her appreciate him even more.

"You have no idea how many ways you've saved me," she said, turning around to face him. "Sometimes I feel like this is all one big dream. Like God is playing a trick on me, and I'm going to wake up and this will all be over. I know I don't deserve you...I don't deserve this."

The breeze blew her hair across her face. Corey traced the outline of her face and pushed her hair behind her ear.

"You do deserve it, all of it," he told her. "You can't change your past, and I would never hold that against you. I love you for who you are; every last speckle of your being. Most times, I feel like you know me better than I know myself. I need that, ma. I need you."

Trina smiled. She had never taken any man for anything more than dollar signs. With Corey, she encountered feelings she never thought were possible. She thought she loved Buttah, but when he took Keilani from her, that love transformed into repugnance. However, with Corey, she was open and didn't mind it. In fact, she welcomed the feeling.

She leaned up and kissed him on his soft lips. "My purpose in life," she said as their lips parted.

"Huh?"

"You asked me what was on my mind. I was trying to figure out the reason for my existence in this world, and I think you've just answered it."

Corey lifted her into his arms, and she wrapped her legs around him. They kissed each other passionately as Corey caressed the small of her back. Then he turned to carry her back inside the beach house.

"Wait," Trina said with a seductive look on her face. "It's perfect out here."

Corey looked around, knowing exactly what she meant. The beach was empty. Only the people who occupied the row of beach houses had access to the area. Corey continued to kiss her as he lowered her body down to the sand. Rising back up on his knees, he took off his white linen button-up shirt, then leaned down and started to massage her perky B-cups with his lips. Her nipples hardened through the black bikini she wore under the thin wrap. He lifted her top, exposing her brown nipples, and took one of them into his mouth. Trina caressed the top of his head as his tongue traced down to her stomach. He circled around her belly button and down to her bikini bottom. He gripped them with his teeth and maneuvered them off of her body with the help of her lifting up. Burying his face into her pussy, he inhaled her scent like it was a drug…and for him, it was. He sucked on her wet pearl, sending Trina's body on a lustful roller coaster ride. She threw her head back into the sand and her back arched up. Deep moans from the both of them colliding with the roaring ocean created its own little melody.

Falling deeper in ecstasy from Corey's head game, Trina tried to hold her nut back. Corey could tell she was fighting the urge. He knew her body too well.

"Let it out, ma," he said in between the swirls his tongue made around her kitten.

Her juices were already quenching his thirst, but he wanted it all. He slipped his tongue and two of his fingers inside of her, stroking them in and out, causing her body to shake uncontrollably.

Trina let out a load moan and tried to grab hold of the sand, which only slid through her fingers. Unable to hold off any longer, she released her juices, and Corey's tongue was there to catch every bit.

"Lay back," she told him. "I want you to feel how I'm feeling right now."

Following her instructions, Corey rolled over to his back. He propped up on his elbows to watch his woman go to work. Trina's head game was one of a kind. She licked his rock-hard dick through his linen pants. His dick pulsed in excitement.

"Oh, he can't wait, can he?" Trina joked.

She undid his pants, pulled out his nine-inch penis, and took him into her mouth with no hesitation. Her head bobbed up and down as she looked up at him. Watching him watching her turned her on even more, and her love box began to beat again.

"Get on top, ma," Corey told her.

Trina gave one last hard suck before climbing on top of him. She slowly lowered herself down on him and his dick slid right inside, filling her up perfectly. Trina removed the top to her bathing suit and the wrap so she was completely naked. She rocked her hips slowly, getting into the motion. Corey palmed her ass cheeks and spread them apart so he could go deeper inside. Trina's rocking began to speed up. She felt his dick hitting deeper, and each time sent a tingle up her spine.

Corey gritted his teeth while continuing to hold on to her. They breathed heavier as Trina rode his dick. Corey dug his feet into the sand and pumped from the bottom. Trina dug her nails into his chest when she couldn't keep up with his pumps. He grabbed her waist and pumped deeper and deeper, faster and faster. Trina gave all the way in and let him take control.

"Oh God, yes," Trina yelled.

Their bodies tightened up almost at the same time, and they both let out a loud moan when they reached their pinnacle. Corey released everything inside of her. She collapsed on his sweaty chest as they both tried to catch their breath.

When his cell phone rang, he reached over and grabbed his pants to retrieve it. He looked at the screen, and seeing Silas's name, he sent it straight to voicemail.

"Who was that?" Trina asked, still lying on top of him.

"Nobody important," he said, then kissed her forehead. "Come and take a shower with me."

Without saying a word, Trina got up and grabbed their clothes. Naked and holding hands, they walked back to the house, where they retired for the evening.

Silas disconnected the call just as Corey's voicemail came on. He tossed his phone on the coffee table of his living room. He wanted to piece together the information he had gotten from Khalil last night. The name Kino didn't ring any bells with him, and he wanted to run it by Corey. They hadn't had beef with anyone because everybody was getting money; at least he thought they were. Silas tried to think of anyone who had it out for them, but no one came to mind. He picked up his phone and dialed Corey's number again, but still got no answer.

Fuck it. Whoever this Kino nigga is, he's going to have to come a little harder if he's trying to fuck with our shit. I can handle this while C is gone. No need to rattle him up about the small shit.

Next, he dialed Khalil's number and waited for an answer. He got Khalil's voicemail after a few rings.

"What da fuck! Ain't nobody answering their phone?" he said, while scrolling to Wayne's number.

"Yo, you at the spot?" he asked when Wayne answered. "How's it looking out there? ... Khalil out there wit'chu? ...Why the fuck that nigga not answering his phone? ... A'ight bet, I'll be down that way in about an hour or two. One," he said before hanging up.

He got up from his leather sectional and headed to the bathroom to prepare for the day.

Wayne hung up his phone and tucked it back into his pocket. "That was him right there. He said he'll be through here in a few hours," he informed Khalil.

"Man, that nigga was on some ole other shit last night," Khalil said. "He been like that since his pops killed himself. Drinking was the way he dealt with it."

"That shit was crazy," Wayne said. "The way he came through here looking for you, I thought some shit was about to go down."

Khalil shook his head. "That's my boy and all, but I can't rock with that shit no more. Fuck this bum-ass hustle they got us on. I'm thinking about going back to the A."

"Word?" Wayne asked.

Khalil nodded. "I'm tryna get this paper, and obviously, they not seeing to it that we all get up. I got to make my own moves."

"You told Silas?"

"Not yet." Khalil took a sip of his Mountain Dew. "But, I'ma let him know."

"Yo." Wayne nodded towards the bottom of the steps.

Khalil turned to see what he was talking about and spotted Kino walking up the block.

"This nigga again?" Khalil said in a low tone to Wayne. "This nigga's on some fed shit."

"Good day, gentlemen," Kino greeted.

"I thought you said you'll be back on Monday?" Khalil said as he stood to his feet.

"I'm not the type to let a nigga know my every move. Being too predictable is a fast way to get a nigga caught up. You'll find that out, though," Kino schooled him as he approached. "I figured you only needed a day to pass along the message."

"Yeah, I let him know what's up," Khalil said as he looked up and down the block, not making any eye contact with Kino. "And we don't know what you talking 'bout, my nigga."

Kino nodded. "What I'm talking about is this money," he said sternly, then reached into his pocket and pulled out a card with his number on it. "I'm not into the cat and mouse game. Tell your boy to call that number tonight."

Khalil took the card and looked it over. "Yeah, a'ight," he replied casually.

"Don't hand me the bullshit," Kino told him. Kino read him like a book and knew he had no intentions on passing the number to his boss. "He got you out here to work, so do what he pays you to do. Make sure I get that call tonight."

Without any goodbyes, Kino turned to leave, got into his car, and pulled off. Khalil looked at Wayne and put the card in his pocket.

Moments later, Silas pulled up. Khalil still had little ill feelings towards him, but wanted to talk to Silas anyway. So, he headed down the steps and got into Silas's car before he had a chance to get out.

"What's good wit'chu?" Silas asked when he saw the look on Khalil's face.

"I need to holla at you," Khalil started. "I've been thinking, and I think it might be best for me to go back to the A for a lil' while."

Silas turned up his face. "For what?" he asked, shutting off the engine. "We getting it out here and you're ready to just leave?"

"No," Khalil said sternly, "you're getting it out here. I'm tired of waiting for another nigga to give me a handout. I need to make my own moves."

"So what, you're going to go back home and be on some boss shit?" Silas teased. "Is that what you think? Corey runs that shit, too, and if you're not with him, then you're against him."

"Yo, what the fuck is going on with you?" Khalil snapped.

"Me?" Silas questioned. "Nigga, you're the one talking about leaving the team."

"Is that what this is?" Khalil cut his eyes at Silas. "You've been about yourself ever since we got out here. You ain't looking out for nobody but Silas. You acting like we wasn't in this shit together. You wouldn't even know how to grind if it wasn't for me," Khalil replied.

Part of what Khalil felt was jealousy. Khalil was the one who introduced Silas to it all, so he felt their roles should have been switched. The other part was ego. Even though Khalil still had a lot to learn, he was tired of Silas's reckless ways and felt he would be better as one of the top niggas instead of Silas. No matter where it stemmed from, what Khalil said was the truth, and he knew Silas needed to hear it.

A disgusted look grew on Silas's face. "I'm the one who's letting you eat out here, ain't I?" Silas said arrogantly.

Khalil clenched his teeth to control himself. He didn't know what was going on with Silas, but he was way out of order.

"I'm out, fam." Khalil pulled out all the work he had on him and tossed it on Silas's dashboard. Then he turned to get out the car.

"If you rolling solo, then I suggest you relocate," Silas said coldly. "I can't control what happens to a nigga taking food from another man's plate."

Khalil's blood boiled from the threat that left Silas's mouth. The thought of causing harm to his friend had never crossed his mind until now. The fact that Silas felt as though he had enough clout to make those types of threats fed the beast brewing in Khalil. Friend or no friend, putting a number on somebody was the ultimate blow. Nobody was going to stop him from getting money, and Khalil knew that sooner or later, they would have to face each other for good.

Chapter 9

"Whether you want to hear it from me or not, it is something you need to know."

"They are so tiny," Angel said to Pablo, as she gently rubbed one of her daughter's hands through the hole in the side of the incubator. Her one finger barely fit in the palm of her daughter's hand.

Pablo stood behind her rubbing her shoulders. Angel looked through the glass and admired them. She hated to see so many tubes and monitors connected to them, but she knew they were the only things keeping her babies alive. She had waited so long to finally meet them, and it killed her not being able to hold them. She wished things were different, but grateful for them to be alive. She never understood what a mother's love felt like until she laid eyes on them. She developed a connection with them while they were still growing inside of her, but to actually see and touch them put a whole new meaning to life.

"When will I be able to hold them?" she asked the nurse.

"Only time will tell," the Middle-Eastern nurse responded. "They're still very fragile. Their lungs are not yet strong enough to work on their own."

Tears formed in Angel's eyes. She loved them more than life itself and would give her last breath if it meant they would survive.

"I know you can do it. I'm counting on you," she said as if the babies understood her.

"Come," Pablo said, "let them rest."

Angel looked up at Pablo from the wheelchair she sat in. She touched his hand that rested on her shoulder and nodded. As much as she wanted to stay by their side each minute of the day, she couldn't ignore the fact that she herself needed rest. Her body felt weak, and she was mentally drained. She looked back at her girls one last time before leaving out of the room.

Pablo escorted Angel back to her room and helped her into the hospital bed.

"Are you alright?" he asked, stroking her hair.

So much was going through Angel's mind at once, from Meeka to Mac and all the other crazy shit that had happened in her life. Seeing her babies fueled the guilt she had about Meeka, and it also made her angry all over again what Mac had done to her. Now that she was a mother, she couldn't imagine putting her kids through the hell that Mac put her through and what she would do if the shoe was on the other foot with Pablo. She had her children, but the thought of losing them broke her heart. A dry lump formed in her throat as she let the tears flow down her face.

Pablo kissed the top of her forehead, which made her feel even worse.

This man has been nothing but good to me. What am I supposed to do? We have a family now. I can't mess that up by telling him the truth, but I don't know how much more of this I can take. Would he even forgive me? Why would he forgive me?

With the thoughts flooding her mind, a piercing pain shot through her temples. She reached up and massaged both sides of her head.

"Do you need anything?" Pablo sincerely asked.

"I have a little headache, that's all," Angel whispered. "I just need to get some rest."

"You rest," Pablo told her. "I'll be back in the morning, but if you need anything tonight, you call me."

Angel kissed her husband and watched as he walked out of the door. She grabbed the remote to the flat screen mounted to the wall and turned on the news. The volume was low, but she didn't plan on watching it for long. Her eyes started to get heavy as she read the captions that popped up on the television screen.

Her eyes slowly opened and closed as the sleepy feeling took over her body. She got one last glimpse of the TV and her eyes shut.

Angel suddenly opened her eyes back up when an image of her best friend Monica's face flashed through her mind. She thought she was dreaming, but when she looked at the TV, Monica's face was there.

She searched the bed for the remote and turned the volume up.

"...she is believed to be armed and dangerous. If anyone knows of her whereabouts, please call your local authorities."

Angel's mouth formed an O shape in disbelief of what she was seeing. She caught the tail end of the newsflash, but the screen read *Incarcerated woman escapes from Cambridge County Hospital.* She hadn't seen Monica since the day in the gym when she found out about Monica's drug habit. She didn't know what happened to her after that, and now she assumed Monica must have went to jail shortly after.

Angel shook her head and lay back in the bed. She felt bad for Monica, but had her own problems to worry about. She wasn't one hundred percent sure if their friendship stood through the test of time anyhow. They had been apart for so long, and when they were finally reunited, it was only for a short period of time. The universe brought them back together, but added the complications to their friendship. The nephew and daughter of the man she loved died at the hands of the man her best friend had given birth to. Her life was complicated, but she realized she and Monica had grown up and a lot had changed. She often wondered if things would have been different if she would have killed Iras instead of Loyal. At the time, she had no idea she and Pablo would come as far as they did. Her loyalty to Monica spared Iras's life, but Angel regretted it. She would give anything to make it right, even kill. She had to do what she felt was right.

Iras killed Trey and Kino killed Meeka. Friend or no friend, they both deserve to die. And when they do, I can finally be at peace.

****

Monica awoke on the moving Amtrak train en route to Atlanta, Georgia. She looked around at the other passengers and down at her cell phone. She had been sleep for the past four hours. She didn't know why she would get so sleepy at times, but she got the best sleep she had in a long time.

"Excuse me?" Monica called to a young woman sitting nearby reading a book. "Where are we?"

"We just stopped in Jacksonville, Florida," the woman responded. "Now we are headed to the final stop in Atlanta."

"Thank you," Monica said and the woman returned to her book.

Monica stared out of the window watching the land pass by. The view looked peaceful, and it reminded her of a place she created in her mind. When she was a little girl, her father told her that whenever she felt scared and alone to close her eyes and imagine she was in a place where no one could get to her. It was her happy place where she would often visit when life got too chaotic. Before the drugs, she reverted to that place where she could run free and no one could follow her there. No cares and no worries; pain didn't exist in that place. It kept her grounded, and she was free. Everything about that place was magical, and everything was perfect until she forgot how to get back to that place. It was a place in her mind that only she knew of…only she held the directions. She became lost and alone inside of herself.

That was around the same time when her life took a turn from bad to worse, and she lost everything she had ever known. Monica learned a long time ago that nothing, even family, lasted forever. The only one that was there for her was an image she had created that lived inside her mind. That image looked exactly like Monica, except her eyes were black as if she had no soul. She was the only person Monica confided in. She introduced Monica to a pure white treat by the name of Cocaine and opened Monica up to a world she never knew existed.

For a little while, Monica thought she found her way back to her happy place because the cocaine made her feel just as good. It temporally took her pain away. They would get high together like there was no tomorrow. The higher she got, the less pain she felt. Eventually, Monica wasn't feeling the effect of the coke, and she needed to add something to her high.

The friend in her mind slowly began to take over. She gave Monica certain orders, and Monica did what she was told. The things she told Monica to do got worse with each request. Monica protested from time to time, but she always lost those inner battles. Monica soon became numb to any feelings. Her mind was already corrupted, controlled by a force she had let in and willingly handed over the keys to the ship. No matter how hard she tried to fight it, she couldn't help but to give in. She did what her friend told her to do and didn't think twice about it. The adrenaline rush she got from her twisted lifestyle was better than the high she got from the cocaine. Mix them together and Monica had the best of both worlds. Causing pain and misery in the lives of the people who hurt her was pleasurable…more pleasurable than sex. She was a psychopath.

****

Pablo arrived at his New Jersey gated home estate after being at the hospital all morning with Angel. It was only late in the afternoon, but he decided to cancel his plans and head home for the rest of the day. He punched in the code at the front gate, drove up the circular driveway, and parked his car.

He unlocked his door and opened it, causing the alarm to sound off. Pablo deactivated the alarm and headed to his first floor home office. As he took a seat at his desk, he loosened the top button of his shirt. He closed his eyes and laid his head back on the leather office chair. He sat quietly, something he liked to do from time to time to collect his thoughts. It was his way of meditating, calming his mind, and being one with the different flows of energy that lingered around him. He took in deep breaths, taking in the positive, and exhaled, releasing the negative.

Pablo opened his eyes when he heard the buzzing of the intercom system. He got up from his chair and looked out his office window that faced the front of the house. He wasn't expecting any visitors, so the pop-up visit made him apprehensive. Looking toward the front gate, he squinted his eyes and saw the figure of a woman standing there. He couldn't make out who it was from the distance. She hit the buzzer again.

He walked back to his desk and pressed the silver button on a small monitor that sat next to his computer. The black and white screen came alive, and Pablo's eyes widened when his eyes saw the face of his surprise guest. A face he purposely hadn't seen in a very long time... Meeka's mother. He stood for a moment scowling at the screen.

TAMMY CAPRI

This cannot be, he thought in disbelief. A look of displeasure took over his face as a rush of mixed emotions hit him like a hurricane.

Pablo slowly reached for the talk button on the intercom and pressed down until a red light came on and a beep emitted from the device. He held the button down without saying a word.

"Hello?" her voice said through the intercom speaker.

To him, that word *hello* echoed loudly in his ear. His heart thumped along with the echo as he glared at her on the screen. It was such a familiar voice to him. He could have picked up her voice in a loud crowded club. Her voice was like venom to his ears.

"Pablo, I know you're there. I saw you go in. There's something I need to tell you, and whether you want to hear it from me or not, it's something you need to know," she said sternly.

Pablo let go of the button. *What could she possibly have to say to me after all of these years?* he thought.

His heart raced inside his chest. He swore that once he put her out of his life, he would never see her again. Besides Angel, she was the only woman that captured his heart. He looked down at the buzzer that would allow her through the gates. His finger twitched as he hesitated to let her in. He slowly eased his finger to the buzzer and pressed it. He watched her on the monitor as she walked through the gates. He walked to the front door, reached for the knob, and slowly turned it. He opened the door just as she was about to knock. A lump formed in his throat as he stood in front of the woman he once loved, but betrayal tore them apart.

"Why have you come here, Tanya?" Pablo spitefully asked.

Tanya removed her sunglass from her face. She was the spitting image of Meeka, thin and tall just like her daughter. Her long, jet black hair was pulled back into a ponytail.

"We need to talk," Tanya responded, while staring him in the eyes. "Can I come in?"

"What could we possibly have to talk about now?" Pablo asked.

"It's about our daughter—"

"My...daughter!" Pablo spat through his teeth.

The longer he looked at her, the more his anger built up. Old feelings resurfaced. He hated her, and to him, she was dead.

"You gave up your rights the day you walked out of her life...our life!"

"You put me out of her life, Pablo," Tanya shot back. "She will always be my daughter, even in death." Tanya's eyes watered. "Now, I didn't come here for this. It took everything in me to come here. You need to know the truth about what happened to *our* daughter. Now are you going to let me in or not?"

Pablo paused briefly as he battled in his mind whether or not to let her in. Finally, he slowly stepped to the side, and Tanya stepped into his home. Pablo closed the door and waited for her to continue.

"There's a lot I have to tell you," she said. "I think we need to sit."

"I'm fine right here. What do you want?" Pablo's tone was cold.

"Fine." Tanya reached into her black shoulder bag and pulled out a purple book. "I'm moving back to Miami, and I found this while packing up my house. It's Meeka's diary."

A look of confusion spread across Pablo's face. "Meeka didn't even know you were still alive, so what are you talking about?"

"She knew, Pablo," Tanya said. Tears cascaded down her face. "She needed to know who her mother was. For years, I had to watch her grow up from a distance. Every dance recital I was there. Every graduation I was there." Tanya's voice choked. "And when they buried my baby, I was there. I just had to know her, to touch her at least once. I waited until she was old enough to understand, when she could make her own decision. So, the night of her senior prom..." Tanya paused as she reminisced back to that day. "She was so beautiful. I followed her...and when I told her who I was, she flipped out on me. But, I thought that was more than worth it instead of living in a shadow."

"No," Pablo austerely uttered. "Meeka would have told me."

"I asked her not to," Tanya continued. "She reached out to me about a week after, and besides the time when I gave birth to her, that was the best day of my life. She got a chance to know who I was...to learn about another side of her that she never knew.

When she went off to college, I moved near there to be closer to her. Now that I had her, I wanted to spend every minute of my day with her. She moved into my house her second year in college."

Unable to hold in his anger any longer, Pablo charged at her. He gripped Tanya up by her arms. "What did you tell her!" he furiously shouted. "How much did she know?"

"I told her the truth!" Tanya yelled back as she yanked away from his grip. "I wasn't going to lie to her anymore. She was old enough to know. She had the right to know that her uncle, your brother Juan, is her real father!"

Pablo grabbed his hair. "Why would you do that?" He paced back and forth. "I raised her! I was the one there when she was born."

"I'm not ashamed of what I've done," Tanya cried out. "I loved you, Pablo, but my love wasn't enough for you. You wanted it all, when the only thing I wanted was you. You couldn't give me that, but Juan was there."

"He was my brother, Tanya!"

"I didn't know what I was thinking at the time," Tanya confessed. "All I know was that it felt right with him."

"He is dead because of you!" Pablo cried out, then punched the front door. Tears flowed down his face like a waterfall. "I killed my own brother...because of you."

"I didn't make you do that. Do not put Juan's blood on my hands!" Tanya hysterically cried. "Your jealousy drove you to do that."

Tensions were high and emotions were in overdrive. A decade's worth of pain was released, and the encounter was like therapy for the both of them. Pablo never forgave himself for killing his brother. As much as he blamed Tanya for it, he knew it was all his fault. He snapped, and he had been begging God for forgiveness ever since. What hurt him more was the fact that Meeka knew he wasn't her real father, but he would never get the chance to explain things to her. Part of him was relieved because he didn't know how he could even come out to tell her. She was his baby girl, and he loved her from the day he first laid eyes on her.

He closed his eyes as he briefly tried to get his thoughts together. Then he looked back at Tanya.

"If your reason for coming here was to open old wounds, then you can let yourself out," he said before pushing past her. He went into his office and sat back down at his desk.

Tanya followed him and tossed the book on his desk in front of him. "I thought you should know about the person you married."

Pablo's eyes widened. "What about my wife?" he asked angrily.

"Read it and then ask her," Tanya said as she put her glasses back on. "If you don't, then I will." She turned to walk out of his office and out the front door.

Pablo heard the door slam shut. His heart beat nervously as he stared at the purple book, wondering what Tanya was talking about.

He reached for the book and opened it to the first page. A few pictures fell out of the book and onto the floor. Pablo sat the book back on the desk and reached down to pick them up, when a picture that had fallen face-up caught his attention. His eyebrows frowned and curiosity struck when he saw Meeka posing in the picture next to Kino. He remembered his face from the meeting they had the previous week in Atlantic City. He picked up the picture and scanned over it, wondering how they were affiliated. Knowing there was only one way to find out, he grabbed the diary and opened up the gateway to Meeka's mind.

Chapter 10

"She wasn't doing shit for him when I met him otherwise he wouldn't have come to me."

Khalil stood in the hotel elevator waiting to reach his destination. He had both of his hands tucked into the pockets of his Adidas track jacket, and his fitted hat almost covered his eyes. His leg jerked nervously at what he was about to do, but curiosity sparked his interest. He glanced at himself in the mirror that covered the walls of the elevator. Never in a million years did he think he and Silas would have a fallout the way that they did. Money and power changed people, but he always thought when it came to them, loyalty would outweigh anything. However, Silas made his statement loud and clear.

The elevator door opened up at the fifteenth floor of the Embassy Suites. He stepped off and pulled out the card he had written the suite number on earlier that day. *1530.* He walked down the hall until he approached the right suite. Khalil knocked on the door and waited for someone to answer.

"You made it," Kino greeted when he opened the door. "Come on in."

Kino extended his hand to Khalil, who shook it and walked into the suite.

"I have to admit," Kino said as he shut the door, "I didn't expect to get that call from you. I ain't think ya boy Silas was the type to send somebody else to his meetings."

"Yeah, well," Khalil looked around the large suite, "this ain't really any of Silas's business, if you get my drift."

Kino nodded just as Iras entered the room. "This is my boy, Iras," Kino introduced.

Khalil nodded to acknowledge him and Iras returned the favor.

Normally, Khalil wouldn't be caught dead going alone to link up with niggas he didn't know, but he was long overdue to step from under Silas and make his own paper.

What the fuck I got to lose? If these niggas on some bullshit, I'll be back in the A anyway.

The guys took seats around the table by the suite's large window. Kino pulled a blunt he had rolled up earlier from behind his ear and a lighter from his pocket. When he lit the blunt, the aroma of the weed filled the air. He took a puff and held it out to Khalil, offering his generosity.

"I'm good, fam," Khalil said, declining.

"A'ight, so what's up?" Kino asked as he blew the smoke out of his lungs. "Why are we here and ya team don't know anything about it?"

"It ain't no team," Khalil calmly responded. "It's just me."

"You was just working that crib yesterday. What, you was just doing them a favor?" Kino sarcastically asked.

Khalil sat up in his chair and rested his arms on the table. "We had our differences. I just decided to do my own thing."

"Ya own thing?" Iras cut in. "You got a spot on a team that's beastin' the city right now. Why would you want them as competition?"

Khalil looked over at Iras. "Any nigga that's so willing to go outside the family and get it on his own only means two things: either he's a grimy-ass dude or the general of the team ain't feeding his soldiers right. So which one is it?"

"One thing about me is that I'm a loyal nigga," Khalil said. He kept his voice calm, making sure he wasn't disrespectful, but stern enough to let them know he wasn't about playing any games. "I don't expect you to believe a word that comes out of my mouth, but I don't do much talking. So, you can decide for yourself."

"Good, 'cause I don't trust no one. At least we have that understanding—" Iras was interrupted by the buzzing of his cell phone. He pulled out his phone, and after looking at the screen, he excused himself from the table and disappeared into another room.

"So here's what it is," Kino started. "We was tryna put ya boy on to a better product at a cheaper price. I know he's coming out of his pockets a grip for what he's copping. But, copping from us would have worked in everyone's favor." Kino finished the last of his blunt and put it out on the table. "But, I only reach out once before having a change of heart. Since he acting like he a *boss*, I'm going to see how much of a boss he really is."

"Well, with all due respect, why not just do it that way in the first place?" Khalil asked.

"We're not about stirring up unnecessary mayhem. We know they're getting money in this city and we ain't knocking that. We want everybody to eat so we don't have to worry about having another cat like you looking for another litter box. Money and respect are two things a man will kill for, and if you're giving it, you will have the most loyal troops in your camp."

Khalil nodded. He felt exactly where Kino was coming from and respected his way of seeing things. Khalil could tell Kino wasn't much older than him, but he talked as if he was a *G* in the game.

Intrigued, Khalil asked, "So what would I have to do?"

"Since you're already familiar with the operation they are running over there, you need to pay a visit to every house they got." Kino looked him in the eyes as he gave Khalil orders. "Our work needs to be flowing from those cribs. They work for us now, and if anybody objects...well, you seem like a smart dude. I don't think I have to explain the rest."

Khalil shook his head. "I knew this shit was too good to be true," he said. "I can be a corner boy back home in Atlanta. I'm not trying to move backwards by working on the block."

"Who said anything about working on the block?" Kino leaned back in the chair. "I'm talking about working *the* blocks, being the face of this takeover. A face these streets will respect." Kino slowly reached out his fist and held it towards Khalil. "So, if you're ready to make this money..."

Khalil gaped at Kino's fist. Some would say Khalil was a rat, but anybody in his shoes would have done the same thing. Khalil made a fist and connected it with Kino's, sealing the deal. Everything about this deal felt so wrong but right all at the same time, and the fact that Khalil was about to step it up made it all worth it to him.

"Now that's what I'm talking about." Kino stood up from the table. "I'm going to get at you tomorrow with further instructions."

Khalil stood to his feet. "A'ight, cool." He slapped hands with Kino before leaving out of the suite.

"Meeting over already?" Iras asked as he entered the room.

Kino nodded as he grabbed bottled water from out of the mini refrigerator.

"What he say?"

"That nigga with it," Kino said in approval. "He just might be exactly who we need, too."

"And if he's not?" Iras questioned.

"I've already prepared to fix it if he ain't."

Iras had reservations about Khalil, but he trusted Kino enough to trust his instinct. If Khalil was a snake, it would only be a matter of time before Iras sniffed him out anyway.

"Well, you get everything set up," Iras told him. "I need to head back home to check on Loyal and Nijah. I'll be back in a few days. Just keep me informed about ya boy."

****

The day had retired and the night ruled the sky. Pablo hadn't moved from his office since Tanya left. At almost one o'clock in the morning, he had read through half of Meeka's thick diary. He hadn't even stopped to take a bathroom break. There were so many things he didn't know about Meeka. It was as if he were reading about an entirely different person. From her first experience with cocaine to the secret abortion she had in her senior year of high school, Meeka didn't hold anything back in her writing. Pablo didn't want to believe what he was reading, because it was a reminder of how much he wasn't in her life. Yes, he had provided a good home and lavish lifestyle that every parent would dream of having for their children, but that lifestyle required money and lots of it. Therefore, Pablo traveled a lot during Meeka's upbringing, and he hired a nanny to look after her until Meeka was old enough to look after herself. His trips in and out of town gave Meeka the freedom to explore the world without any guidance, and for a young girl, that was a dangerous combination.

Besides finding out Meeka's secrets, he hadn't read anything pertaining to Angel. He had gotten as far as Meeka's new male friend by the name of D-dos. He turned to the next page and continued reading.

April 2, 2011

Maybe it's me. Maybe I'm the one that's tripping. Yeah, he kept it real and told me that he wasn't looking for anything serious, but that nigga wasn't acting like it at all. Shit, he treated me more like wifey than he did his own bitch. Now it's "we're spending too much time together" and he needs to breathe. Who the fuck does he think he's fooling? He really must think I'm one of these average bitches out here. D-dos got me fucked up if he thinks he can just drop me like a bad habit for another bitch. What makes him think she's going to step up her game now, anyway? She wasn't doing shit for him when I met him. Otherwise, he wouldn't have come to me. No, I'm not tripping! He is foul for the way he's treating me. I've been nothing but patient with his ass, and yet, he still hasn't returned any of my calls or emails. I got something for his ass, though. I wonder how wifey would take it if she found out his ass got another baby on the way. Humph! Yeah, it's fucked up to lie about shit like that, but so the fuck what. He brought this on himself. That'll teach him to play with somebody's heart!

The ringing of his cell phone diverted Pablo's attention. He reached for it and sent the call to voicemail without checking to see who was calling him. He wasn't in any mood to speak with anyone. He felt he was one step closer to finding out what happened to Meeka, like she was reaching out to him in death to lead him to the clues. His gut feeling was telling him that what he needed to know lied in her diary. He had a one-track mind, and that was to get to the bottom of his daughter's death.

He turned his cell phone off, tossed it on his desk, and flipped to the next page. He flipped back when he noticed the date had skipped from April 2nd to April 30th, not sure if he had skipped a page or two, which he didn't. Meeka took almost a whole month off from writing in her diary, which seemed unusual for someone who was consistently pouring out her thoughts and feelings. *Something must have happened.* He turned back to the page and resumed his mission.

April 30, 2011

Oh my God! What have I done? Things have gotten out of hand. Nobody was supposed to get hurt. Trey is missing and it's all my fault. I should have never told Trey that D put his hands on me. I should have known how my cousin was going to react. Fuck! What was I thinking? I just wanted D-dos to pay for what he did to me, but things just got out of hand. Now D is dead and Trey may be next. I need to find him. Somebody at that club knows something; it was too many people for no one not to have seen what happened. If anything happens to Trey, I swear on my life that whoever hurts him, I will make sure they burn in hell. God please protect my cousin wherever he may be. I will never stop looking.

May 7, 2011

I am one step closer to finding Trey. I got a job working at Club Heaven. Yeah, it's a strip club, but it was the last place he was at before he disappeared. Desperate calls lead to desperate measures, and this call, I had to answer. He is my blood, and I cannot have his blood on my hands. So far, I've found out there's this guy named Kino. The word is him and his boy Iras knows something about Trey's disappearance. But, a lot of shit you hear in a strip club is bullshit. I think they may know, but I just don't know how much they know. If I work there long enough, maybe I'll get lucky. I don't know exactly what my plan is, but I need to get close enough to Kino to find out. I feel so bad for hiding this from my dad. I've done some crazy shit, but this, he wouldn't be too happy with what I'm doing. This shit is too complicated. The less my father knows the better!

May 9, 2011

It felt good to finally get this off of my chest to another person. I felt like it was just me against the world, but now that Angel is helping me, this shit might work. Angel is some jail bitch that my dad got living with him. She supposedly made a promise to my cousin Theresa while she was locked up that she would help us find Trey. My dad and Theresa trust her, but I'm not sure if I can. But, hey, as long as she helps me find Trey. Angel came up with the perfect plan, too. I could tell she was a scandalous bitch. We are meeting tonight at Club Heaven so I can show her who Kino is and we can get this plan going. I'm going to put it on Kino so good that he'll be ready to wife me. Angel says that no man can resist the power of the pussy, and once Kino is under my spell, he will be singing like a bird. I just hope Angel is as hard as she comes off, but who am I to judge? She's the one who did time for killing her own father. I have yet to end someone's life, but if Kino is involved, he will be my first.

Fuming, Pablo turned to the next page only to stumble on a blank. He skimmed through the rest of the book hoping to find more, but there wasn't. Pablo slammed the book shut and flung it across the room. So many emotions caved in on him all at once. Confused yet enlightened; deceived yet didn't want to jump to any conclusions.

Angel never mentioned any of the things Meeka wrote about. What was the plan? Did Kino have something to do with Trey's death, or better yet Meeka's? Why would Angel not tell me? She's my wife.

171

With so many unanswered questions, nothing made sense. The thought of Angel keeping that from him made him question her intentions. He knew she loved him. He felt it every moment, even when they were apart, but he just could not wrap his mind around the idea of Angel lying to him, especially about Meeka.

She knows how much Meeka meant to me. Angel would never do that.

His thoughts consumed his mind. There was only one person who had the answers to his questions.

I will talk to Angel, my wife. I need to know everything she knows. This has got to be a misunderstanding, I am praying it is.

Chapter 11
The Takeover

"It's all done," Moms said, as she removed the white mask from her face. She smiled in approval of the kilos she just cooked and packaged, ready to go. "Like baking a cake," she added.

Khalil sat across from her at the dining room table. "I'm impressed," he admitted. "Where I'm from coke is cooked by naked young women. I feel like I'm here with my grandma doing this shit."

"I was young and naked back in my day," Moms joked, putting her hand on her hip. "Once you learn how to do this shit, you never forget. It's those young bitches that be fucking it all up. You're gonna need an experienced old hag like me to fix their mistakes."

"And besides," Kino said as he entered the room from the back. "Moms probably taught all these young bitches how to do it."

"Damn right," Moms added as she clapped her hand.

Khalil laughed. "A'ight, Moms, my bad."

"Moms ain't no joke when it comes to this," Kino tested. "She's the truth, for real," he said, then tapped Khalil on his shoulder. "Come on, we got work to do."

Khalil grabbed the duffle bag that Moms prepared from off the table and followed behind Kino out the apartment.

They drove around the city to every trap house that Silas ran. Khalil made sure he left an impressionable message with Corey's hustlers. Khalil knew Corey was out of the country, so it wasn't going to be too hard for them to be convinced. But, Khalil left them with no choice.

They headed over to the last house where Khalil worked, as he filled Kino in about everything from his beef with Silas to Corey bringing his team from Atlanta. Khalil only knew of a few details from what Silas told him. He didn't believe Corey was just going to move in so easily because he knew about the east coast and the infamous Eric Taylor. Eric's name rang bells, even in Atlanta. Khalil spoke about him like he was royalty, which told Kino that the Taylor family still held an impression in the streets. Kino didn't tell Khalil that Eric was Iras's father, because he wasn't sure if Khalil would run his mouth or not, and he knew Iras wasn't ready to let the city know the Taylor clan was back. Kino was still feeling him out. Only time would prove if Khalil was ready for that information.

They arrived at the house. Just as Khalil expected, Wayne was there. Khalil hopped out of Kino's truck and approached him.

"Yo, man, I don't think it's a good idea for you to be around here," Wayne said. "If Silas comes—"

"Man, Silas can suck my dick," Khalil responded with disgust. "I know that nigga ain't got you shook."

"Naw, it ain't even like that. You know you my mans a hunnit grand, but—"

"But what?"

Wayne sighed. "Look, I just don't want any trouble. I'm not getting between that shit with y'all." Wayne looked up and saw Kino get out of the truck and lean on his hood. "Yo, what the fuck you doing with that nigga?" he asked, confused.

Khalil looked back at Kino and then back at Wayne. "Oh him?" He smiled. "That's your *new* boss."

Wayne screwed up his face. "Fuck you talking about?"

"Exactly what I said." Khalil let the smile fade from his face so Wayne would know he was serious. "You work for him now." He passed Wayne a brown paper bag. "That's the only thing that will be coming out of this spot."

Wayne looked into the bag. "Shit," he said when he saw what was inside the bag. He knew at that point, he had no other choice but to do what he was told. Wayne was familiar with Khalil's murder game, and he knew Khalil wouldn't hesitate to pop a nigga in broad daylight.

"Why are you doing this, man? This shit is not going to turn out good."

"Nothing personal, just business." Khalil saw the obvious change in Wayne's expression, as if he knew what was about to happen.

Wayne was one of the good dudes...pretty laid back. He didn't mind working the trap and was only trying to make his money. Khalil knew Wayne was contemplating in his head.

"Man, I don't know about this. This shit ain't right."

Khalil pulled out his pistol and put it directly to Wayne's head. "Well, let me make the decision for you," he coldly said.

Wayne's eyes widened. "Yo, Khalil...chill, man. Don't do this shit, man," he pleaded nervously.

"Like I said before, it's just business," Khalil reiterated. "You're either getting money with us or not at all."

"A'ight, man, you got it," Wayne agreed. "Just put that shit away."

Khalil stared at him for a brief moment before removing the gun and turning to walk away. Halfway down the concrete steps, he stopped and turned back to look at Wayne.

Khalil sent two bullets straight to his head. Screams of nearby pedestrians could be heard as they ran for cover. Wayne's body dropped to the ground as his blood leaked from the bullet holes. Khalil's gut feeling told him that Wayne would be a problem. He had worked with Wayne too long, and from what he learned, Wayne had no type of heart to stand up to Silas. All he would do was be in the way. It was also Khalil's way of sending a message to Silas.

"Goddamn," Kino said as Khalil walked back to the truck.

They both hopped in and pulled off.

Chapter 12

"This is us right here. We did this."

The sound of the reggae mixes from the DJ put a relaxing vibe in the air. The outdoor beach club that Corey and Trina decided to attend was the perfect atmosphere. Trina had retired her clubbing days back in the states. It was like a risk to have fun because hood niggas and alcohol didn't mix. It was bound to be some type of drama that may end up in a bloodbath, and Trina wasn't interested in making the morning news. Without Keilani, it wouldn't have been fun for her anyway.

This club was different. Everyone was dancing and feeling the vibes from the speakers. Being in

Jamaica made her see the world and people a little bit differently. She wasn't used to seeing how everyone mingled so well.

In her white sundress, she swayed her hips to the tunes of the popular hit "Baby Boy" by Beyoncé. Corey held onto her waist as he danced behind her, letting his body flow along with hers. They danced barefoot under the night sky until the song came to an end.

"I don't ever want to leave here," Trina said as she grabbed Corey's arm. "Can't we just get Akahi and stay here forever?"

They walked back to the bar area.

"When the time is right, we can move to any place in the world that you'd like."

"Yeah, but when *will* the time be right?" she sincerely asked.

A dark toned, topless male waiter approached them and placed two tropical-colored napkins in front of them.

"Wa ya drinkin'?" he asked in his heavy Jamaican accent.

"Two Jamaican rum punches—"

"Uh, no," Trina said, cutting Corey's order off. "I'll have water, please."

The waiter looked at Corey, waiting for his drink order.

"Okay, one rum punch then."

"Ya got tit," the waiter said before walking away.

"No drinks for you tonight?" Corey asked.

Trina shook her head. "No. I've felt queasy since lunch. It must be this heat."

"You want to head back to the house?"

Trina shook her head. "No, I'll be fine."

"Well, I need to use the bathroom," Corey said as he stood up. "I'll be right back." He kissed her on the lips before walking away.

"Ear ya go," the waiter said, placing their drinks down on the bar.

Trina nodded and grabbed the glass of water. She took it back in one gulp. *Damn*, she thought. She had never been so thirsty in her life. *This is going to be a long nine months if I'm getting sick like this already.*

Just before they left for Jamaica, Trina took a pregnancy test because she had missed her period. She was going to surprise Corey while in Jamaica.

"Ya need more?" the waiter asked.

Trina sat the glass down and nodded. Starting to feel dizzy, she took in deep breaths, but the humid air did nothing to soothe her. Nausea kicked in, and she wasn't able to hold it in any longer. A warm sensation trickled up her throat, and she brought up everything she had eaten. Corey hustled over as she was bent over hurling on the sand beside her.

"Damn, babe," he said, grabbing a few napkins from the bar and handing them to her.

Trina looked up and saw that a few people had their eyes glued on her. She rolled her eyes.

"Damn, they staring like they've never seen a pregnant woman before," she said loud enough for them to hear.

They must have gotten the point, because as soon as she said it, they minded their own business.

"What did you just say?" Corey asked as Trina stood up slowly.

"You're going to be a daddy." She shrugged.

Corey paused for a brief moment. "Ahhh!" he screamed and then scooped her up in his arms, lifting her off of her feet. He kissed her lips and spun around while he continued to hold her.

"Ugh," Trina said as she pulled her lips away. "You are so trifling. I just finished throwing up."

"I'm going to be a daddy?" he asked, putting her back down. Corey was so excited that he didn't think about it. "Woo, baby, do you know you've just made me the happiest man on earth?" He grabbed her by her waist, kneeled down on the ground, and placed his ear to her flat stomach.

"What are you doing?" Trina laughed. "Get up. You're embarrassing me."

"Baby, you don't have to be embarrassed," he said as he continued to listen to her stomach. "This is us right here. We did this."

Trina smiled. "It's not even a baby yet. What are you listening for?"

"It's my seed and I know she's in there." He kissed her stomach through her dress.

"She?" Trina frowned. "How do you know it's not gonna be a he?"

"Because Akahi is our *he*." Corey looked up at Trina. "And he is going to be the perfect big brother to his little sister."

Corey's words brought tears to Trina's eyes. She always knew Corey loved Akahi, but she didn't think he loved him as much as she did because he wasn't her son. Hearing him speak of Akahi as if he was their son reflected on the type of man Corey really was.

"I was going to wait until we got back to the house to do this." He reached in his pants pocket and pulled out the ring box. "But, right now seems like the perfect time."

Trina put her hand over her mouth. Her eyes widened when she saw the ring box. Corey opened it and held up the ring.

"Oh my God." Trina was mesmerized by the beauty of it.

"Will you be with me for the rest of my life?" He removed the ring from its compartment. "Will you marry me?"

"Girl, ya got chu a gud man, ya hear?" a woman shouted from the crowd. "Just say yeah!"

Trina looked up, and they, again, were the center of attention, but this time, she didn't mind.

"Oh, hell…yes!" Trina laughed in harmony as Corey slid the ring on her finger.

The ring sparkled from the light of the lanterns positioned all around the club. The crowd cheered, and the DJ announced their engagement.

Corey stood up and embraced her. "Come on," he whispered into her ear. "Let's get out of here."

Trina hugged him tightly around his fit waist. She lifted her head from his chest and looked him in the eyes. "Whatever you want, baby. I love you."

****

Silas sat in his car up the street from his South Philly trap house. He watched the house as cops swarmed all over. He went there after visiting his other houses and finding out what Khalil had done. Khalil boxed Silas out. He had gone to see Wayne because he knew Wayne wouldn't turn on him, but instead, he got something he had least expected. Wayne was dead and the house was now under police investigation. Yellow caution tape blocked anyone from going near the house.

Silas got out of his car, walked down the block, and stood in a crowd of people that were gathered watching the crime scene. He was beyond pissed and he was no fool. He knew Khalil was behind it, but he didn't expect for him to take it this far as to kill Wayne.

"If anybody knows any information about what happened here, we're asking that you come forward and help us get to the bottom of this," the police officer said to the crowd as he approached.

None of the people said a word. Even the ones who did know kept quiet. People in the neighborhood knew who Silas was, and his presence there made it even more awkward for some. Silas knew this because as soon as a few of them saw he was there, they left the scene. The majority of Philadelphians knew that snitching was a one-way ticket to get killed, and most didn't talk because they feared for their own safety.

Silas saw Wayne's body lying on the ground covered by a white sheet. Rage filled his body and his finger twitched just thinking about Khalil. This meant war, but Silas was outnumbered. He needed to let Corey know what was going down, and he knew he wasn't going to take this news lightly.

Pulling out his cell phone as he headed back to his car, Silas dialed the international number Corey had given him for emergencies.

Corey sat in the single bamboo chair with Trina straddling his lap. Both exposing their bare chest, they kissed passionately as their skin touched. They left the patio door open so the breeze could hit them and give them a reason to keep each other warm. The house was dark, but the natural light from the night's sky was just enough.

Corey's phone rang.

"Mmm," Trina moaned. "Don't answer it," she whispered in between kisses.

"No, baby, I have to. It might be Si. He's the only one I gave the house number to."

Trina sighed as she got up off his lap. Corey quickly grabbed the telephone by the sofa and switched on the floor lamp.

"Hello?"

Trina stood in front of him with her arms folded across her chest and tapping her foot on the floor. Corey put one finger up as if telling her to give him a minute.

"Yo, Si. What's up?" Corey said. "I was in the middle of something, so this better be important."

Annoyed, Trina rolled her eyes and went into the other room, knowing he would be longer than a damn minute.

"What!" Corey said into the phone. "Run that by me again."

Hearing the obvious change in his tone, Trina popped her head back into the living room. Corey paced the floor with one hand on his hip.

"No," Corey said with nothing but malice in his voice. "Don't make a move until I get there." He slammed the phone down so hard that he cracked the glass of the end table.

"Is everything alright?" Trina asked.

Corey stood for a moment staring into space as he gathered his thoughts.

"Get dressed," he finally said, then walked past her and into the bedroom.

Trina followed him and watched as he pulled their suitcase from under the bed and started throwing their clothes in it.

"We're leaving?" Trina moaned.

Corey continued to pack without saying a word.

"Damn, babe, what the fuck happened?"

"I've got to get back home and fix some shit."

"Fix what?" Trina questioned. She began to get impatient with Corey's secretiveness. "Whatever it is, you mean to tell me it can't wait until our vacation is over?" Trina stood waiting for an answer. "Corey!"

"No, it can't!" Corey snapped. "It's too much shit going on and I will explain later. Now pack your shit. We have to go. Now!"

Trina stormed out of the room and into the bathroom, slamming the door shut. She sat on the edge of the claw foot tub.

I know it has something to do with his street business. I wish he would just leave that shit alone for good. We can't even enjoy a vacation without one of his boys interrupting. She bit her bottom lip and shook her head as her anger grew. *Why is he always putting that shit before us?* She stood to her feet, looked at herself in the mirror, and tapped her finger on the sink as thoughts roamed in her mind. *Fuck it!*

She walked back out of the bathroom and into the bedroom. She flopped down on the bed, grabbed the remote to the television, and pressed the power button.

"What are you doing?" Corey asked.

"I'm staying here, and I'm going to enjoy the rest of my vacation alone," Trina said without looking at him. "If whatever back home is more important than staying here with me, then go. But, I'm staying."

"T, we don't have time for these games," Corey said in a calm tone. "Listen, I'm sorry for yelling at you. I won't let it happen again, but we really have to go."

Trina sat on the bed with her arms folded like a little girl holding a grudge.

"We'll come back," Corey said, walking around to her side of the bed. He sat beside her and reached for her hand. "Or we can go anywhere else you want; I promise you that. You know I would not be leaving if it wasn't important. Nothing is more important to me than you and making you happy."

"Then do it," Trina finally spoke up. "Make me happy."

"Am I not now?" Corey asked.

Trina twisted her lips. "You know what I'm talking about. When are you going to leave these streets alone? I mean, damn, you want to marry me. I'm going to have your child, Corey. We have a

190

family. This shit is not forever. Why can't you go back to teaching at the university? You know, something normal? I just want a normal, happy life with you, nothing more and nothing less."

"I know you do." Corey leaned in and kissed her on the forehead. "And I'm going to give you that. You have my word. In a few months, I'll be done with this shit for good." He held out his pinky finger as he told her exactly what she wanted to hear. Corey had every intention of getting out of the game, but not anytime soon. "I pinky swear."

A smile slowly spread across Trina's face when she saw Cory pouting, poking out his bottom lip.

"You better." She linked her pinky with his, and he pulled her into him and kissed her cheek.

She got up from the bed, walked over to the closet, and pulled out a few outfits she had hanging up. "You are so lucky I love your ass to be leaving this place."

Corey got up and finished what he started. Trina put the clothes on the bed.

"Only a couple more months, then I don't want to hear about this ever again," she said before leaving the room to shower.

LOYALTY II

Chapter 13

"If you're still here when I get back, I won't be
able to control what I do to you,"

"Hey, honey," Angel said into the phone when
Pablo finally answered. She had been calling him for
twenty-four hours and wasn't able to reach him.
"Where have you been? Is everything okay?"

Pablo hesitated before telling her that he was
fine, but Angel could sense he really wasn't. His
awkward tone made her a little worried. She didn't
want to push the issue over the phone, especially
since she was coming home that day. She knew he
couldn't hide whatever it was if they were face to
face.

"They will be discharging me around noon today," Angel continued. "Tango's picking me up?" she asked, confused.

Why would he be sending someone else instead of picking me up himself? He didn't stop by to visit me or the girls yesterday. Something's going on, but I will make sure to find out as soon as I get home.

"Okay, I guess, but are you sure you're okay? … Alright, I'll see you later on. I love you."

The nurse knocked on the door and entered. "Mrs. Gomez?"

"Yes?" Angel sat up in her bed.

"Hi, I'm Nurse Patti-Ann. I'm filling in for your nurse. She had to leave early, but I'll be doing your discharge."

Angel nodded. "How are my girls?"

"They are both coming along quite well," the nurse said as she checked Angel's vital signs. "Another week or so and they should be just about ready to come off of their breathing machines. Lift your shirt for me, please." She put the stethoscope on her ears and placed the other end on Angel's chest to check her breathing.

"When will they be able to come home?"

"Their doctor will be able to give you a better answer," the nurse said. "You can see them once your discharge paperwork is complete." She removed the IV needle from the back of Angel's hand and secured the spot with a gauze pad and medical tape. "Everything looks good. You can get showered and dressed, if you like," the nurse told her, then unhooked the monitors.

"Thank you," Angel said.

After the nurse left out the room, Angel swung her legs over the side of the bed and stood to her feet.

"I can't wait to get in my own bed," she said as she limped over to the closet in the room.

She retrieved the small travel suitcase with her clothes in it that Pablo brought to her. She put it on the bed and unzipped the flap. The first thing that caught her eye was a white envelope with her name on it. It was the first time she had opened the suitcase. She picked up the envelope and opened it. It was a letter from Pablo. She sat on the side of the bed and read silently.

Angel, I love you more than words could ever express. From the moment I saw you, I knew I had to have you. You taught me how to express myself as a true man. You taught me everything I know about loving someone again. In this past year of marriage, our love has only grown. When I am with you, the world and its troubles are nothing to me but a blur. When I have a bad day, I know you are there for me. I'll do anything to make you smile, to kiss your soft, sweet lips, to look into those beautiful eyes that sparkle with happiness for the rest of my life. In those eyes, I see a fire of passion and safeness. I had already given up all hope on love until I met you. Our love is a testimony, and our beautiful children are a reflection of a pure and genuine love. I love you more than life itself. I thank God for the day you were born. –Pablo

Shivers shot through Angel's body as she read over the letter. He made her feel good even when he was not physically there. His words explained exactly how she felt about him, and Angel couldn't ask for more. *I'm coming home to you, Pablo!* A burst of excitement developed in her like she was meeting him for the first time and falling in love with him all over again. She put the letter on the bed and finished getting dressed.

Angel waited in the nursery with her daughters until it was time for her to leave. Tango arrived at the hospital at noon just as Pablo said he would. He escorted her into the backseat of his car and put her bag in the trunk. Holding on to Pablo's letter, Angel read it over and over again the entire ride home.

Tango pulled up to her Jersey home, punched in the code to the gate, and drove her up to the door. Angel had expected for Pablo to greet her as soon as she arrived, but that didn't happen.

"Is Pablo here?" she questioned Tango while getting out of the car.

"As far as I know," Tango replied as he retrieved her bag from the trunk. "He just called me this morning and asked if I could pick you up."

Angel nodded and headed up to the door. She pulled her key from her purse and unlocked the door. Tango followed behind her into the house and sat her bag down by the step.

"Well, I have to make another run," he told her. "I'm glad you are okay."

"Thanks for everything, Tango," she said.

He left out the door and she locked it behind him.

"Pablo?" she yelled out in her luxurious home. "Baby, are you here?"

She walked into his office to see if he was in there. The house was quiet enough to hear a pin drop. He wasn't there or anywhere else on the first level of the house.

She went upstairs and into her master bedroom. "Honey?"

"I'm in here," he said from Meeka's room.

She walked down the hall to Meeka's room and found Pablo sitting on her bed.

"I got your letter," she said, smiling as she walked toward him. "This really made my day. I can't tell you how—" Angel stopped mid-sentence when she saw the troubled look on Pablo's face. "Did something bad happen?"

Pablo cuffed both of her cheeks with his hands and gently kissed her lips. "You know I love you, right?"

"Pablo you're starting to scare me. What's the matter?"

"What I am about to ask you, I need you to be completely honest with me."

"Yes, baby, whatever you want. Just tell me what's wrong," she said sincerely.

"I got a visit from Meeka's mother, and I need to know if what she is talking about is true."

"Meeka's mother?" Angel asked, baffled.

"I will explain it all later, but right now, I need you to tell me what you know about Meeka's death. What happened to my daughter?"

Pablo's voice echoed in her ears after he asked her the last question she had expected. Her heart beat nervously, and the butterflies in her stomach swarmed around inside of her. Her arms filled with goose bumps, and the room seemed as if it were getting smaller and smaller. She opened her mouth to speak, but her voice cracked. Her words were caught in her throat, but she knew she had to tell him the truth. Tears streamed down her face.

"I can't," she cried in a whisper as she lowered her head to the floor. "I couldn't bear the thought of you not loving me anymore."

Pablo dropped his hands from her face. "Angel, what are you saying?" he asked. He had hoped what he read wasn't true.

Angel sobbed and shook her head.

"Answer me!" Pablo yelled, startling her. "What...happened?" he repeated through clenched teeth.

Her nerves jittered as she struggled to get her words out. "When I came here, Meeka told me that she thought a guy named Kino had something to do with Trey's disappearance. I only wanted to keep my promise to Theresa and find out what happened to her brother, your nephew." Angel took a deep, dry swallow. "I came up with a plan for her to get closer to him. She didn't want you to know what we were doing, and at the time, I didn't think it mattered."

Angel stared into space as if watching the past playing out right in front of her. "After a few weeks, Meeka started acting different and stopped answering my calls. She was spending so much time with Kino that she got confused about what she was supposed to be doing. She fell in love with him and it blinded her. She called me one night after we got into a huge argument, the night you and I went out on our first date. I was so mad at her that I didn't answer." Angel let out another loud cry. "She must have been calling for help, because the next morning when I checked my message, I heard her... I heard him... And I heard..." Angel closed her eyes. "I heard him shoot her." She kept her eyes closed because she didn't want to face him.

Pablo backhanded her and she fell to the floor. "Why didn't you tell me!" he shouted.

Angel bawled on the floor. Her face burned from the smack, but she was more shocked that he hit her the way he did. Pablo had never put his hands on her until now.

"I had already fallen in love with you," she yelled. "I was afraid of losing you, of you blaming me for her death. I didn't know what to do, Pablo. I'm sorry."

Pablo was outraged. To him, no woman in the world meant more to him than his daughter, but Angel came fairly close. He looked down at her in disgust as she whimpered on the floor. Part of him felt bad for hitting her because his love for her was strong. He wanted to grab her in his arms and hold her, but the more he thought about her dishonesty, the more his anger influenced his decisions. He reached down, gripped her by the neck, and pinned her against the wall.

"How could you do this to me? To Meeka? You should have come to me!"

Angel tried to release his grip, but he just held tighter cutting off her air supply. "I...can't...breath," she managed to squeeze out.

Pablo released his grip and Angel fell to the floor.

Pablo stood over her breathing heavily. "You have one day!" Pablo said.

Angel looked up, and for the first time, she saw pure hatred in Pablo's eyes.

"Get your things and get out of my house," Pablo said in a low tone. "If you're still here when I get back, I won't be able to control what I do to you," he warned with a cracking voice before he left out the room.

When Angel heard the front door slam, she let out a loud cry. Her life changed in a blink of an eye, but she knew she caused this for herself. Pablo was kind-hearted and gentle with her, but the other side of him turned into a monster. She didn't want to leave her home, but she knew if she stayed, Pablo just might kill her.

I have to make this right, she thought.

She got up and darted out of the room and down the steps. She ran into his office where the key hooks were located. That was the last place she remembered her car keys being, but no keys were on the hook.

I love him. God knows I do. He needs to see that I am still the woman he fell in love with.

She went to his desk and searched around until she found her key in a cup holder. She took her keys, but a photo sticking out the top of a purple book caught her attention. She opened the book and instantly recognized Kino's face in the photo. She grabbed the entire book and left the house. She was determined to fix this and nothing was going to stand in her way.

LOYALTY II

Chapter 14

"Apologize to Buttah when you see him."

"Whoa!" Iras playfully shouted, while lifting his daughter into the air in the living room of his Atlanta two-story single home. Nijah's laugh only caused Iras to do it again. Her laugh brought him joy. He was happy to be home, even though it was only for a short time. He missed his baby girl. He kissed her chunky cheeks and blew on them, making a farting sound. He walked over to the couch, sat on the end opposite of where Melissa sat, and put Nijah on his lap.

"She is so happy to see her daddy," Melissa said. "You know she said da da, right?"

"Word?" Iras said with his eyebrow raised. "You said da-da? Huh, boo? You said da-da?"

Nijah looked at him and smiled the most innocent toddler smile. Iras kissed her again.

"Well, we should get going," Melissa suggested, looking at the time on the cable box. "Visiting hours at the hospital start at eleven, and I know Loyal can't wait to see your face."

"I can't wait to see her," he admitted.

"Here, let me change her so we can go," Melissa said before taking Nijah upstairs.

Fifteen minutes later, they were all ready to go.

"Do you want me to drive?" Melissa offered.

"Yeah, but I'm going to take my car, too," Iras said. "I have a stop to make after the hospital."

Melissa strapped Nijah into her car seat and got in the driver's seat. They both pulled off into the beautiful Atlanta weather and headed to see Loyal.

Monica sat on a bench in the family park behind a newspaper. The park was located across the street at the corner of Iras's house. She had the perfect view of Iras's house from where she sat. She saw both Iras and Melissa leaving the house. They drove past her, and when they were out of sight, she closed up the newspaper and dropped it to the ground. She stood to her feet and made her way to the front of his door. She looked around to make sure no one was watching her. She then grabbed the doorknob and turned it. She knew it would be locked, but it was worth a try.

"Good morning," she heard someone say.

Monica twisted her neck to see who it was, and an elderly woman came out of the house next door. Monica watched as she stuck a key under a flowerpot on her porch.

"Good morning," Monica said back as normal as possible.

The woman walked down her steps and got into her car. Monica looked down on Iras's porch and saw a doormat. Lifting the doormat, she found a single silver key. *Thanks, lady!*

Monica unlocked the front door and put the key right back where she found it.

"I'm home, son," she said out loud with a devilish grin. "Did you miss me?"

Monica was the only one there, but she spoke as if she was talking to him. She walked through the living room and into the kitchen.

"You've been a bad boy, and now Mommy is going to have to teach you a lesson."

She moved around Iras's kitchen freely, as if she wasn't afraid of being caught. The thought of them returning any minute was like food for her adrenaline.

Monica slowly pulled out one of the kitchen knives from its compartment. She looked at her reflection in the knife.

"Ugh," she huffed. "Well, the least I can do is freshen up for you," she said, staring at her own eyes.

She went upstairs as if it were her home and ran the water in the bathtub. She slid off the dress she had worn for the past couple of days and lowered her body into the water. She leaned her head back and closed her eyes as she put together her plans for revenge.

****

"How the fuck did you let this happen?" Corey chastised Silas. "You let another mu'fucka run up in your house and take your shit?"

Corey couldn't wrap his head around what Silas was telling him. Silas told him everything about him and Khalil. Corey paced his living room floor, something he always did to keep from snapping on someone.

"Look, C, we can fix this shit," Silas assured. "I will personally handle Khalil's rat ass myself. I'll rock him to sleep on sight."

"No," Corey said. "Take me to him. I want to show him what happens to a rat."

Trina stood at the top of her stairs listening to their conversation. She couldn't help the tears that freely flowed down her face. She had a gut feeling things were going to get bad. Hearing the front door shut, she ran down the steps and followed Corey outside.

"Corey!" she called out just as he and Silas were getting into the car. "Don't do this. You don't have to do this," she cried.

"Trina, not now, okay?" He opened the car door.

"If you get in that car, I'm leaving," she threatened. "Me, Akahi, and our baby are leaving. I will not raise my kids around this. It will never end because you won't let it."

Corey paused for a brief moment. He looked at Trina before getting into the car. Trina's heart shattered. Her world caved when Corey chose to leave. She watched as he pulled off and then went back into the house.

Red flags instantly went up in Kino's head when he saw Trina coming out of Corey's house. He and Khalil were parked a few doors away. Khalil showed him where he lived, and when they spotted Silas's car parked outside, Kino wanted to keep a close eye on them. He got more than what he had expected.

"That's Corey's bitch," Khalil explained, not knowing that Kino was already acquainted. "She bad, ain't she?"

They both watched her as she went into the house.

Kino maintained his stare as suspicions cluttered his thoughts. To him, it wasn't any coincidence that as soon as Buttah was dead, Trina popped up with the same niggas that took his place in the drug game. Something was fishy, and when Kino got that feeling, he was prepared to reel in the big one.

"Yo, Khalil, tell me again," Kino said. "How did Corey move his team over here from Atlanta?"

"I don't know exactly, but when the word got around that the Taylor family was no more, next thing I know, we came over here," Khalil said. "It almost seemed like an overnight success; something that was way too good to be true. I wouldn't be surprised if Corey had parts in taking them out."

"Grimy bitch!" Kino said, as the last piece of the puzzle snapped into place. "She set him up."

Kino grabbed his gun and hopped out of the car. Khalil had no clue what was going on, but he followed suite with his gun in hand.

Kino kicked in Corey's door and invaded his home.

"What the fuck?" Trina yelled as she came down the steps. "What—" She froze halfway down when she saw Kino standing in her living room with his gun pointing at her.

"You set him up," Kino said.

"Kino what are you talking about?" She asked nervously. What are you doing in my house?

"You know what the fuck I'm talking about!" he spat. "You set Buttah up."

"No," she shook her head. Her fear was at an all-time high. It felt as if her heart had sunk into the pit of her stomach. Her mind told her to run but her legs wouldn't move. The tears slid down her face as she began to plead for her life. "You've got to believe me, Kino. I would never do that to Buttah."

I would never do that to...I would never do that... the words echoed as distorted flashed backs of Meeka saying those exact same words the night he killed her flood his head. He slowly blinked his eyes and when he opened them, he saw Meeka was standing there instead of Trina. Hell unleashed inside of him and there was no turning back.

"Die, bitch!" Kino fired three shots.

"Ahh," Trina screamed as she ran back up the steps.

The gunshots rang loudly in her ears as the bullets chipped away the wall. She managed to dodge the bullets. Kino followed behind her upstairs into a bedroom.

"Kino, please. No, don't do this," Trina pleaded.

Kino grabbed her by the hair and hit her across the face with the butt of his gun.

"I should have known it was you," Kino shouted. "You set Buttah up."

"No, I didn't," she cried with blood leaking from her mouth. "I had nothing to do with that. Please," she pleaded. "I'm pregnant."

Kino's ears were deaf to her cries, because in his mind, she was guilty, and all he saw was blood. "Apologize to Buttah when you see him."

Kino sent two bullets to her stomach. He looked into Trina's face as she struggled for her life. Images of Buttah flashed through his mind. He was going to shoot her in the head like they did Buttah, but he wanted her to die a slow and painful death so she could think about what she did.

Confused, Khalil stood behind him and watched the whole thing go down. He didn't know how ruthless Kino could get, but all the doubts he had were confirmed at that point.

They left the house, got back in the car, and pulled off.

"What was that shit all about?" Khalil asked.

"Just so you know," Kino said, keeping his eyes on the road, "the Taylor family isn't all dead, and we're taking back our empire."

Khalil's eyes widened. "You mean—"

"Ras is Eric's son," Kino told him.

"You're fucking with me, right?" Khalil said.

Kino didn't respond.

"You're serious," Khalil concluded. "Oh shit!" He heard many stories about them, but never did he ever think he would be a part of their team. He was ecstatic inside and pleased with the decision he made to call Kino that day.

"It's a lot I'm going to fill you in on," Kino told him. "But, first, we need to get this nigga Corey out of the way for good."

****

Damn, Corey thought as he drove down City Avenue. He was on a murder mission, but all he could think about was Trina. He let his ego block his view of the love he had for her. What he had to do was important but not worth losing his relationship over. The look she had painted on her face when he left the house hurt him to his heart. *If the tables were turned, I know Trina would have never second guessed it.* He made a U-turn and headed back towards his house.

"Si, can you look for these niggas solo?" Corey asked. "I need to get back to Trina, but call me as soon as you find them."

"No problem," Silas said. "You good?"

"I hope so," Corey said. "I can't let her walk out of my life over something stupid."

Silas nodded and Corey burned rubber back to his house.

"Why the fuck is your door wide open?" Silas asked when they pulled up to Corey's house.

Without saying a word, Corey flew out of the car and ran up to his house. He hadn't even cut off his ignition. He knew Trina wouldn't have left the door open if she had left, so he automatically thought someone intruded. He ran in the house with Silas following closely behind.

"Trina!" he called out. His eyes caught sight of the bullet holes in the wall. "Oh shit."

He panicked as he rushed up the steps.

"Trina!" he called again, but still no answer.

He burst through his bedroom door and froze.

"Oh shit," Silas said when he got to the door.

Trina was lying on the bed covered in blood. The sight was gruesome.

"Oh my God!" Corey rushed to her side. "No," he cried out. "Who did this? I was only gone fifteen minutes."

Silas didn't know what to say. He watched as Corey lifted Trina to his lap. He was hysterical.

"Come on, baby. Wake up, please," he cried. "I'm sorry, baby. I love you. I'm sorry. Just please wake up."

It was no use; Trina was already dead.

Chapter 15

"It's the World Series."

Loyal and Melissa sat in the lounge area of the head trauma unit. They visited just about the entire day, and Iras took Nijah to get something to eat in the cafeteria. Loyal's progression was steady, but she still could not walk on her own. She spent all of her time in bed or a wheelchair. Melissa was just glad she was a fighter and things were finally looking up. Everything about the day she had been shot was still a blur to her, but some of the doctors said she may unconsciously choose not to remember it. The brain has a way of storing things away for good.

"Where is he with the food?" Loyal asked in a slurred, slow voice.

Melissa laughed. "I don't know why you're asking. You know you're on a liquid-only diet."

"That's why I'm still fucked up," Loyal joked. "I need some real food."

Melissa laughed again. "At least your sense of humor is not fucked up."

Loyal didn't have full control of her facial muscles, but Melissa could see the slight smile on her face.

"Mel," Loyal said, "if I haven't told you already, thank you."

"Girl, you don't have to thank me," Melissa said. "I'll just put it on your tab," she joked.

"I'm serious. Thank you for being such a good friend. You are always around when I need you. The doctors tell me all the time how lucky I am, and I find myself counting my blessings. Every time I do, you come to mind."

"Now why are you trying to make me cry up in this place?" Melissa said as her eye ducts filled with tears.

"Because I don't think I could have gotten through the last few years without you. I appreciate that more than you know."

Melissa reached over and hugged her. "I love you, too, girl." The tears came down her face. "And I'm going to always be here for you. I know if it was me up in here, you would do the same thing. You're my sister. We don't have to be blood; our loyalty makes us sisters."

"Somebody is knocked out," Iras said as he entered the room carrying Nijah, who was sleeping.

Melissa looked up. "She done ran around so much she wore herself out. It's her bedtime anyway." Melissa got up from the chair. "I should get her home and in the bed."

Iras kissed Nijah on the forehead and handed her over to Melissa. She grabbed the baby bag off the seat and swung it on her shoulder.

"Alright, honey, I will see you tomorrow," Melissa told Loyal before kissing her on the cheek. She lowered Nijah so Loyal could give her a kiss, and then, she made her way out.

Iras took a seat on the end of the couch closest to Loyal's wheelchair.

"How long are you staying?" she asked him.

"As long as you want me to." He smiled.

"Don't ever leave me, okay?"

"It was never an option," he said, rubbing her hand. "Well, if I'm going to be here a little longer, let's go back to your room. You should be resting anyway."

Iras stood to his feet, took the brakes off of her chair, and pushed her to her room.

The sun had just started to set when Melissa arrived back at the house. She looked in her rearview mirror at Nijah. *Good*, she thought, *she is still sleep.* She loved Nijah, but she was definitely a handful, and Melissa took advantage of all the free time she got.

"Time to curl up to some *SVU*," she said as she got out of the car.

She grabbed Nijah and walked in the house straight to the nursery. She lay her down, stripped her down to the pink onesie she had on underneath her clothes, and turned on the baby monitor.

Melissa then went into her room and flicked on the light. She grabbed her robe from the closest and tossed it on her bed. She began to undress so she could shower before her show started. Just as she put on her robe, she heard Nijah on the monitor sitting on her dresser.

"Damn," she said.

Melissa tied the robe's belt in front of her to keep it closed. She walked in the room and stood over the crib.

"You know you're sleepy, so we are not going to fight tonight," she said to Nijah. She picked her up and sat in the wooden rocking chair to try and get her back to sleep.

Monica watched her from the slightly cracked closet door inside of the baby's room. Melissa sat with her back facing the closet. It had been a long awaited moment for when she would see her sister again, but this reunion would certainly be the best of all time...well, at least for Monica. She slowly opened the closet door, making sure she didn't make a sound. She walked out of the closet, lightly taking each step. She got closer and eventually stood directly behind her. Monica tightened her hand around the knife she had grabbed earlier from the kitchen. She slowly lifted it into the air. *I am going to enjoy this.*

****

"Umm," Loyal moaned.

Iras opened his eyes. He had fallen asleep in the single hospital chair in Loyal's room.

"What's wrong?" he asked.

"I don't know," she said. "I got this weird feeling all of a sudden."

"You need me to call the nurse?"

"Yeah," she said. "Maybe the pain medicine is wearing off. I just feel weird."

Iras pressed the nurse's call button on the remote. He looked at the time on his phone and saw all the missed calls from Kino.

"Damn, I must have been tired," he said, stretching. "I didn't even hear my phone ringing."

The nurse knocked on the door. "Did you need anything?" she asked, walking into the room.

"She said she thinks her medicine is wearing off," Iras told her.

"Okay, well, I will see if it's time for her to get more," she said before walking out of the room.

"Did Melissa call you?" Loyal asked. "She usually calls when she gets home."

"No. Only calls I got were from Kino."

"Maybe you should call her. Just to make sure she got in safely."

The nurse walked back into the room. "Okay, I can give you some Morphine. You want that?"

Loyal nodded. The nurse began to put the medicine in her IV line.

Iras walked to the top of the hospital bed and bent over to kiss her on the lips. "I got to go. I will be back first thing in the morning."

"Don't forget to call Melissa," she reminded him.

"I won't," he said. "I love you."

"Love you, too."

As Iras walked to his car, he dialed Kino's number. He got into his car and pulled out of the parking garage. Kino didn't answer.

"Yo, Kino, my fault. I was knocked out. Call me when you get this message," he said into the phone before hanging up.

It took him no time at all to get home, and it was a good thing because he was beat. His body felt worn out, and he was definitely going to enjoy a good night's sleep. He got out his car and went inside the house. None of the downstairs lights were on, but he saw the light shining down the steps from upstairs. He cut on the lamp that sat on the side table next to the couch and tossed his car keys on the coffee table.

He headed upstairs to Melissa's bedroom. Her lights were on, but she was not in there.

"Yo, Lissa?" he called out, but didn't get an answer.

He walked into the baby's nursery and saw her sitting in the rocking chair. The back of the chair was facing the door.

Damn, she must have been sleepy to fall asleep in here, Iras thought.

He walked up to the back of the chair and tapped her shoulder. It wasn't until he got closer that he saw the blood covering the front of her robe. The only light in the room was from Nijah's nightlight, but he knew what it was.

"Oh shit!" Iras yelled. "Melissa?" he shook her hoping that she was still alive.

Melissa's head slowly tilted forward. It rolled down her body and on to the floor.

Ira's eyes widen in shock. He stood there in disbelief of what he had just witnessed. It was like a scene straight from a horror movie.

His heart skipped beats as he stared at Melissa's decapitated body. He quickly thought of Nijah. He rushed to the crib looking for his daughter. He searched through the blankets, pulling them up, but the only thing he found was a note.

You want your daughter? Then give me your bitch! 404-859-2717.

"No!" he snarled through his teeth.

So many emotions hit him at once. He didn't know who it could be because he didn't have any problems with anybody in Atlanta.

"Who would want to kidnap my daughter? This has got to be a mistake."

Looking at the number again, he realized it was Melissa's number. He ran downstairs to get his phone and dialed the number.

Monica gripped the steering wheel tightly as she sped down Route 85 in Melissa's car. Nijah was sleeping soundly in the backseat. Blood still covered her hands and clothes from the massacre she left behind. She didn't bother to clean herself.

When Melissa's cell phone rang, she took one hand from the steering wheel and grabbed the phone from the cup holder. A devilish grin spread across her face when she saw Iras's name.

She pressed the speaker button. "Hello, son." The phone grew silent, but Monica could still hear breathing. "How have you been?" she said in almost a seductive tone.

"Monica, where is my daughter?" Iras said through the speakerphone. "I swear if you hurt her—"

"You're gonna do what?" Monica cut him off. "I didn't think so," she said when Iras didn't say anything.

"Now, you listen to me," she demanded. "If you want this baby back, then you have to give me another life…Loyal's life! You can have Loyal or your daughter, but you can't have both."

"Why are you doing this? Give me my daughter!" he spat.

"You heard what I said. Now you've got to make a choice, and if you think about calling the cops, she's dead."

"Monica!" Iras said as he started to lose his cool. "You crazy bitch! This isn't a fucking game!"

"Ha," she laughed. "I know. It's the World Series."

LOYALTY II

ABOUT THE AUTHOR

 Tammy Capri hit the literary scene in 2012 with her debut novel *Loyalty*. Tammy was born and raised in Philadelphia, Pa. She has always had a creative side that surfaced at in early age. Her love for the creative arts has led her down a path to be a published author.

In 2003, she attended Cheyney University and received a BA in Communications.

In 2006, Tammy became a member of Delta Sigma Theta Sorority Inc. She released her sophomore novel, *The Mobster's Wife*, in September 2012, and a short story E-book series, collaborating with two other authors, in November 2012 titled *Hush Money*.

At 27, Tammy is a wife, mother of two handsome boys, the founder of Nu Class Publications, and she is ready to take her writing career to the next level. With a promising future ahead of her, Tammy Capri is sure to become a household name!

LOYALTY II

www.ingramcontent.com/pod-product-compliance
Lightning Source LLC
Chambersburg PA
CBHW020326200626
46814CB00006BB/2439